Elkhorn Mountain

by
Willis Carrico

PublishAmerica
Baltimore

First printing

PublishAmerica has allowed this work to remain exactly as the author intended, verbatim, without editorial input.

ISBN: 1-60672-163-1
PUBLISHED BY PUBLISHAMERICA, LLLP
www.publishamerica.com
Baltimore

Printed in the United States of America

Elkhorn Mountain

Dedication

This book is dedicated to all our forefathers who fought for a better life for the future generations. For the people that we have long forgot, who plowed this land and made a living from this good earth. For the hardships of the many men, women and children that slaved to make this country great. It is to these folks that I dedicate this book.

Signed,

Willis Carrico

Introduction

Thomas Bach climbed the cobblestone stairs leading to the main part of the jail. The dim light from the street lamps followed Thomas as the stairs wrapped around the building. This walkway led him to a large wooden door with solid steel plate hinges. Thomas stared at the door wondering who might be behind it and what road or path this day would bring.

Thomas had worked for the Montana Star newspaper for nine years and this was his first really big assignment. His task was to interview the man that they would hang, at dawns first light, for murdering four men and two women on Elkhorn Mountain.

Thomas pushed open the wooden door and a cloud of old foul smelling air hit him in the face, sending Thomas staggering against the stone wall. As he stood there, raw stagnate water started to seep into his brown leather shoes and the sounds of yelling came from down the slightly lit stone hallway. "What have I gotten myself into?" he questioned. Thomas turned and stared though the open door behind him. "Should I leave and act like this day never happened?" he thought to himself. But then he started to think about his duty at the newspaper and the nine long years of writing about the weather and every boring story the paper had given him. Turning and holding his handkerchief to his face, he started to walk down the hall. "I will do this. I'll just write a short page or two, then I'll be done and I'll never come back," Thomas thought to himself.

Contents

Chapter One
The Interview

Thomas slowly walked down the hall and he noticed some light shining ahead of him. Just then a tall man dressed in a military type uniform approached him. The guard drew his weapon on Thomas and yelled, "Stop and give your name!"

"Thomas… Thomas Bach. I'm a writer for the Montana Star newspaper. I am here to do an interview with Regan," Thomas explained.

"You're here to see Regan, no one sees Regan," the guard laughed.

"I have all the papers and they are in order. They are signed by the warden." Thomas handed over the papers to the guard. "And here is letter from the warden saying that I have been commissioned to write Regan's side of the story on this date, May 15th, 1885," Thomas said.

The guard looks over the papers and handed them back to Thomas. "Well, Thomas it's your funeral." Then the guard turned and started to walk down the hall on the left side. "Follow me but walk on this side of the hall. The cells are on the right and sometimes the prisoners want to reach out and...well... you'll see what I mean in a moment," the guard said.

As they walked down the hall they came upon the first cell. Thomas looked in and saw a huge man laying on the bed with his back toward him. Thomas figured this man must weigh at least four hundred pounds. "What did he do" Thomas asked the guard. "This is Alex Keller. He murdered old men by slashing their throats and then taking over their homes and land," the guard explained. "He's due to hang next week. Thomas passed several other cells but didn't ask anymore question. Finally they came to another large wooden door. The guard yelled "Place your hands though the hole, Regan. You have a visitor." Just then two very large hands appeared in the hole in the stone wall. The guard placed cuffs with chains on them on Regan's wrists. "Now go stand with your face toward the wall," the guard ordered. The guard drew his weapon and unlocked the four locks and then swung open the door. He ordered Regan to sit on the bed and place his hands on the sides of the bed. Then the guard ran a heavy chain through the holes in the bed and then to Regan's legs. "Now, Mr. Bach, if you have any trouble just yell. I won't be far and if Regan is bad he just might not make it to morning." With that the guard exited and for the first time Thomas got his first really good look at everything.

The bed was made of rusted pipe and the mattress hung to the floor as Regan sat in the middle. Thomas looked at Regan noticing he wore no shoes; his pants were in tatters and his white shirt torn, dirty and hanging open in the front. Regan's face was weathered and his hair was unkempt, but when Thomas looked into his eyes they were empty. They had no compassion, no life, no fear. "You can tell a lot about a man through his eyes" Thomas thought. Regan stood at least six foot six inches tall.

Thomas placed his papers on an old wobbly table, but he kept watching, his eyes on Regan. Thomas was so caught up in Regan that when he spoke, Thomas nearly jumped. In a deep raspy voice Regan spoke for the first time, "You have papers for me to sign." At this point,

Thomas tried to regain his composure and told Regan, "I'm Thomas Bach, a writer from the Montana Star and I am here to write your side of what happened on Elkhorn Mountain" Regan's face fell into his hands and silence fills the room. Then slowly a small sound came from Regan's hands and then the sound of laughter filled the room as Regan's hands reached upward,,, "Your what?" Regan questioned "I'm Thomas Bach and I'm…" Thomas is cutoff in mid sentence. (Regan voice changes from laughing to loud and hard) "What the hell are they doing to me, like I want to spend my last hours with a guy from a newspaper that will take everything that I say and turn it around for his dollar and make me out to be something that I'm not," Regan ended.

"Mr. Regan"

"Regan is my first name you idiot. Everyone calls me Regan but my full name is Regan P. Wright. You can make a note of that if you want." Regan laughed again.

"Regan, if you please, It is my intention to write your side of the story and yours alone. The information will be collected, examined and processed, but it will be what you tell me." Thomas explained. With that Regan looked Thomas over from head to toe, shook his head, looked at the floor, and then there was a long silence. Thomas took out his ink, quill and paper and waited for Regan to start. After five minutes or so, Regan looked up at Thomas. Thomas now noticed that Regan had changed from when he first entered the room. Regan now looked calm. Regan then asked Thomas, "Where would you like me to start?"

Thomas smiled and said, "Well, from the beginning would be nice. I'll have questions, but just carry on, Mr. Wright. Carry on"

Regan took a deep breath and began "It all started two years ago from July. I had just sold my farm before the bank took it and had a few dollars left over. I was livin' in Mitchell, South Dakota. I took a job with a local man, Jim Fulton, on his farm as a handyman. They were real nice folks, good people. I was fixin' fences, breaking horses and doing anything else they needed done for the farm. Then one Sunday afternoon, a wagon full of people pulled up to the main house and everybody went inside. They acted like they knew each other so I didn't think much of it and went back to doing my work. A few hours later, Jim, the man that I took the job from said he had to talk to me over supper, about something that might interest me. Well, that night the dinner was huge. I mean meat and potatoes, even cake with frosting. I sat down at the table and was introduced to Jim's company. He started with his brother Lyle, then Lyle's wife Mary, Lyle's older son Bob and Lyle Junior. Then his daughter Joyce, her husband Tom and lastly their youngest daughter Jill, there were six in all. I introduced myself. We said grace and started to eat." At this point Thomas noticed that Regan started to stare out the small window.

"Please continue, Mr. Wright," Thomas said.

Regan continued, "After dinner the men went to the front porch for a smoke and the women cleaned up from dinner. Then Lyle started to ask me some questions about my travels." Regan stopped and a silence ensued while Regan looked down at the ground.

"What kind of questions?" Thomas asked.

"Well like how far west had I gone and if I had seen any of the last Indians, stuff like that. I told him that I had been well west of the Bitterroot Mountains in Montana, and that in my younger days I had rode with a pretty ruff crowd." A smile rose on Regan's face, "It was then Lyle that asked me if I had ever been to Elkhorn Mountain, Montana. I said yes and then I started to ask him questions. I asked him why he was asking all the questions and it was then he said he wanted to hire me on as a guide. He said he wanted to go to Helena first to take care of some business, then it would be off to Elkhorn and that he would pay me $500.00 for my trouble." Thomas's jaw dropped open, "$500.00 is a lot of money for a few hundred mile trip. What all did you have to do?" Thomas questioned.

Regan looked right into Thomas's eyes, "I would have to give them safe passage through 'til they reached Elkhorn. Cook, hunt, guide and if necessary, kill to protect his family. That's when Jim spoke up. He said he would keep my job for me and that my work would be waiting for me when I got back. I then looked at Lyle and asked him when he was leaving? He told me without skipping a beat that he would commence in the morning. Jim came over and said that he would consider it a personal favor if I did this for his brother. So after thinking about it I said yes and went and started packing."

"So you never thought this through too much, did you?" questioned Thomas

"Looking back, I should have just saddled up and rode off. No, not much thinking was involved when you're talking $500.00," Regan smiled again.

Thomas looked at his watch. An hour had passed since he had came into Regan's cell. Then without asking, Regan started up again. "In the morning I said my goodbyes to Jim and his family and I headed out with Lyle and his family. We stopped in a town called Norton and got food, water, ammo and a few extra horses. It was then I was approached by the local sheriff."

"The local sheriff... did you have a past with him or was he wishing you well?" Thomas asked.

Regan stood up and stretched out his arms as far as the chains would let him and stated, "No, he just wanted to know where we were headed and I told him the whole story. It was then that the sheriff walked up to Lyle and they started talking. I was tethering everything down and after a few minutes I noticed that they started to get loud, I walked to the front of the wagon to see what seemed to be the problem. The sheriff just walked away shaking his head and saying something under his breath. I asked Lyle what was wrong, but he just said that the sheriff and him never got along. It was at this point that Lyle handed me $100 in gold coins. I just stood there looking at the gold. It was more money than I had ever had at one time. He told me I'd get the rest when the job was done."

Regan looked down at his right hand as he told this part and then looked up catching Thomas off guard. "You could have just walked off and never looked back. Why didn't you? Thomas asked.

"Because $500.00… it could give me a new life, a new start. It could set up a new farm and I could settle down. Did it change my life?, Yeah it did, but it did for the worst." Regan stated as Thomas took off his glasses, cleaned them and then put them back on. He then looked at his watch. It read 3:15. "Only a few more hours," Thomas thought to himself.

Thomas looked at Regan and he started again. "We headed out and rode all day and stopped only when dusk fell. By the time I bedded down the horses and got supper cooked it was midnight. This went on for several days. We crossed into Pierre, then into Spearfish before entering Montana.

We saw no signs of Indians or any trouble what so ever. But when we went through a small town called Chester, the town was gone. Empty, just like an ole' ghost town. This town gave off a bad feelin', the kind that runs down your back. We rode through and that's when I first noticed it. Hundreds and hundreds of arrows. They where stuck in the houses, doors and watering troughs. They were everywhere. I got off my horse and walked over and pulled an arrow out of a door. I had seen one like this before. My grandfather had a collection of arrows and he showed me the difference in each one. CROW, I yelled back at the rest of the wagon. Lyle came over and looked at the arrow and asked me what I thought it meant. I told him this town was taken over by the Crow Indians and that it looks like sometime last winter. When the food gets low, the Crow will kill for whatever they need. We need to keep going and find a town to bed down in for the night. We crossed over 12 miles and, as night fell, we could see the lights of a town just ahead. We pulled into the town and Lyle took his family to the Hotel while I settled the horses at the stable. As I went into the stable, the stable hand met me and said that it would be 25 cents per horse for food and water per night. He told me his name was Jack… Jack Nice. A short, old little fella, that walked with a slight limp on his right side. I thought he was making it up, but he had a name tag and everything... "Jack Nice Stableman, it said."

Anyway I asked Jack about the town of Chester and he just laughed, said it had been dead for over a year now. The Crow had wiped it out, killing men, women and children. Stole the entire town in the dead of night. He also told me that his sheriff had issued a telegram to all towns in a four state area warning travelers not to come through Chester. It was then that I wondered if this was what the little talk was about between Lyle and the sheriff of Norton.

Jack and I unloaded the wagons and bedded down the horses. I paid him for one nights stay. It was now time for a drink and to relax. I entered a rough house saloon. It was just me. Plus four other men that were playing cards at a table near the bar and the bartender. I ordered a beer and one of the men asked me where I was from and where I was going. I told him Elkhorn Mountain. He got a strange look on his face and asked me if I was sure I wanted to go there. I told him I was being paid to take two wagons and one family to Elkhorn and we were too close to turn back. Another man spoke up and said, "I hope you're carrying enough guns to get through the Gulch Creek passage. The Crow have been hanging around there running wild. A bunch of Crow left the reservation and, well, you can see what they did to Chester. I asked the men about the army. Would they give us safe passage though Gulch Creek? They laughed and good said luck finding the army. I knew at this point that we had to come up with some other plan. I drank my beer, paid the barkeep and went to get a room.

As I walked into the hotel, Lyle was standing talking to three other men and he waved for me over. Lyle said that these men would be riding to Elkhorn as hired guns. I told Lyle and the three men what the other fellas had said in the saloon. Lyle then told his men that it was imperative that they arrive in Elkhorn before the next two weeks. He would pay a bonus to each man if they stayed. They shook hands and Lyle said he would see everyone at breakfast around 6am. With that they all left. I got my room and went upstairs. I opened my door and layed down on a mattress, not a hard chunk of dirt, but a real mattress. I sank into that mattress like a rock on water.

I was awakened in the morning by Jill. She tapped on my door and said it was 5:30 and that I needed to wash up for breakfast. I really didn't want to move. Lying on a fine mattress was hard to give up when you're looking at laying on lumps of mud. But I got up and washed in the basin and felt clean and fresh. I got dressed and went downstairs to a grand breakfast. Lyle had ordered a large meal for everyone. (eggs, bacon, ham, bread, milk), fit for a king. I ate like a pig. When everyone had eaten, Lyle stood up and held up his drink and said, "Onward to Elkhorn." We loaded up and pressed onward. I kept a good eye on the new men at my side. This was the first time I had gotten a really good look at these men. All three were rough around the edges. Their skin was darkened by the sun and their faces were older with lots of wrinkles. They didn't say much as we progressed west, which really was a good thing.

Helena, Montana was only a week away but we had yet to cross through Gulch Creek Pass. Gulch Creek played heavy on my mind. I set up the wood for the fire for the night and put on the kettle for beans and bread in the pots. The fire licked up the sides of the main kettle. Darkness fell and everyone gathered around the fire and ate. No one talked to anyone, and then I heard a sound coming from the horses. I put my plate down and crossed over the side. That's when I saw them. Crow braves trying to steal the horses. I yelled for everyone to come. Everyone came carrying a gun and shot at the braves. The Indians ran to their horses, yipping and screaming. I yelled for everyone to stop shooting. I looked at the horses. They were all there and laying on the ground was a young Indian brave, shot in the back. The Fultons all gathered around the brave. I told everyone I would take care of this in the morning. I went back to where the boy was laying, wrapped him up in a extra blanket that I had and placed him beside my spot by the fire. I stared at the fire not really looking at it but through it. This boy was much too young to have died this way. No one deserved to die with a bullet in their back. It was about this time that Joyce and Jill came walking up to me.

"What are you going to do with him?" they asked.

"In the morning I'll find his people and return him so his family can bury him proper. It's the right thing to do. Don't worry. They will be watching us tonight. Try to stay together; the men carrying guns in plain site. That should keep them at a distance."

"I don't think anyone got any sleep that night. If they did it was few and far between. I'll even have to admit, I slept with one eye on the young brave.

In the morning I loaded up the brave on a horse and headed over the hill. I left all my guns at the campsite and only took a water canteen. I had ridden about 2 miles when I heard them, they were riding fast. I stopped, held up my hands and just waited. I was hoping that if I gave them back their brave they might give us passage through Gulch Creek pass."

This whole time Thomas was writing as fast as he could, while Regan rested laying down on his side. Thomas looked at his watch, 4:10, if Regan was going to finish this story, he had better hurry. "O.k. Regan continue please." Thomas said looking and waiting for Regan to tell the next part of his story.

There were 10 or 12 of them and they lead an extra horse. They lined up in front of me and one of them gave a younger brave some order, he got off his horse and walked over to the dead brave. He grabbed a hold of him and placed him on the other horse. The older Indian slowly walked his horse up to me. He stared at me looking deep into my eyes. Then he spoke, "We thank you for returning my youngest son. He will be a hero to his people. These times are hard for both the red and white man. Old ways are hard to change. Are you headed west?' I told him my name and yes we would be taking the trail to Gulch Creek Pass., then to Helena and from there to Elkhorn. "You carry no gun." Then he started to talk to two young braves. One brave picked up his war lance from his shoulder and walked his horse toward me. I stood my ground. The brave looked into my eyes but his stare was different. Did he want something or was he just going to kill me. He stopped beside my horse and jammed the spear into the ground. The older Indian spoke, "this life spear will get you through to the end of Gulch Creek Pass, after that you are on you own" and with that they rode off.

I followed my trail back to the campsite carrying the lance. When I rode into camp, Lyle came running up to me, 'They're gone. They're all gone.' Lyle explained that when they all woke up the three gunmen had gone in the night. Then he thought I had also left he was pretty upset. I explained where I was and about the spear. We packed up and rode down the road leading into Gulch Creek Pass."

Thomas rubbed his eyes and spoke, "This truly is an amazing story, Regan. So now you're getting close to the journey's end, what are you thinking?"

"Well, I was thinking mostly on how I was going to spend that money. As we rode through Gulch Creek Pass, from the corners of my eye once in a while I could see the young Crow braves. They would hide behind trees and rocks. There was no doubt that they were following us. I was hoping that they would leave after we got through the pass. Inside the last mile of the pass, we set up camp for the night. I couldn't wait 'til this whole thing was over so I could stop cooking for these people. After two weeks it was getting really tiresome. After dinner Lyle came up to me and told me he really was thankful for all I had done for him. He also gave me another hundred dollars in gold coins and said that he would not finish out on the payment once we reached Helena, but would pay me at Elkhorn. He left and I couldn't help but think how strange this family was. I mean, I barely talked to any of the family the whole trip. They definitely were a quiet bunch and stayed in the wagons just about all the time. By midday the next morning, we were out of Gulch Creek Pass which was good and bad. Good that we had crossed it, but bad that we didn't have the protection of the Crow anymore. Helena was only three days ride away, then five days until Elkhorn and then find a good place to settle down."

"Sounds like you're winding down Regan," Thomas said looking at his watch. "Its 5:20; they will be coming soon."

"Yeah I would hate to keep anyone waiting. The hair on my back stood up again about 3 miles outside of Helena. We bedded down for the night. Lyle and his family took shelter in the wagons and God unleashed his fury on the mountain. I ran in my tent and the rain fell in buckets, I mean, water was spraying everywhere, and you couldn't hear a thing with the thunder. This lasted most of the night. In the morning the hair on my back was still standing on edge. I awoke to the fresh smell of the morning and we just ate jerky for breakfast and headed on into Helena.

When we came into Helena, we must have been a site. We looked like about ten miles of bad road-dusty, dirty and in need of a bath. We unloaded everyone and Lyle said that everyone needed to meet back in three hours. I knew exactly what I wanted to do. Get a bath and a good meal. I stabled the horses and headed to the bathhouse (25 cents for hot water, 35 cents for soap and hot water).

I had just sat down in a tub full of hot water and was enjoying the heat and relaxing for the first time in a long time. The door opened and the local sheriff and two men entered the room. The only thing they asked was, "Where did you get the spear that you left with your horses." I told him about what had happened and he warned me not to get to comfortable with the Indians. He said that they would kill me if given a chance. Then the sheriff leaned down and whispered to me, "Watch who your friends are" and with that the men left. I finished bathing, dressed and headed to the hotel that I saw when I came into Helena. It had a sign saying, 'Home-Cooked meals'. At this point that sounded mighty good to me. During dinner I thought about what the sheriff and his men had told me. I'm not much on being scared by anyone-let alone the local law.

After dinner I looked at my watch and found I had another hour to kill. So I stopped by the general store and picked up two pairs of jean and a new shirt. Later I found my way back to the wagons to meet back up with the Fultons. About ten minutes went by and as I waited I noticed several pairs of eyes watching me through the side-street I was facing. It was then that I saw Lyle walking across the road carrying a steel box with a padlock on the front. In a very strange voice Lyle said it was time to go. I gave him a look of all right let's go. I pulled back the wagon cover and the family was all there waiting to get started. I thought, well, we just got here but at least I'm clean and have a full stomach. With a slap of the reins the horses tore down the main street of Helena and off to Elkhorn Mountain at last.

It was two days later when that strange feeling came on me again. As night fell from the twilight skies, I could make out a few figures on horse back riding over the ridge. Not Indians, but more or less trouble anyhow. I watched them until it got too dark to see. They crossed over onto the main trail and gently vanished into the woods. I stayed up most of the night, propped up on a large rock next to the fire. I kept thinking that in the morning we would start our climb up Elkhorn and then it would be over. Looking up at the stars that were just coming out, I could hear the Fulton family getting ready for bed. The sky was bright and alive, with just a hint of fall in the air. It was early September in Montana and I thought how it would start snowing in five short weeks. I looked over to where the men had caught the main trail. Maybe the cowboys were just behind us and there was nothing to worry about, except I still had that feeling. I sat on that rock and the last thing I remember, I was thinking 'It's almost over, it's almost over.'

I woke to the dawn where the sun light was just cresting the mountain ridges. Jerky for breakfast again this morning, but that just meant we could get this day over with and a day closer to journey's end. We rode to the base of the mountain and crossed over onto the main trail. As we climbed the mountain, Lyle kept stopping and opening that steel box he had. He'd look at this paper, use his compass and then we'd move on. We only got five miles up Elkhorn on this trail when night fell. That strange feeling I had was now in my stomach also. I just couldn't shake it off. We unloaded and set up camp. I had a nice fire going and started to cook supper. As the water got hot, I could hear thunder on the horizon. The night sky was clear. Must be heat thunder I thought. I shook it off and went back to cooking supper. For the first time on the entire trip the Fulton family asked me to stay and eat with them. We sat around the fire and really talked. They wanted to know everything about me and my background but there wasn't much to tell. We talked into the night. One by one they excused themselves and went to bed. In the end it was just Lyle and me sitting by the fire.

We weren't talking much, when Lyle got real serious he got up from where he was and sat down beside me. He asked me if I was wondering what was in the steel box. I told him if he thought I should know, he would have told me. He laughed and got up and got the box and set it down beside me. He then opened his shirt and around his neck was this key. He took the key and opened the box and started to show me everything. The box contained a compass, eye scope, bag of gold containing $700.00 and a map. Lyle unwrapped the map and it showed another trail that branched off from the main one. This other trail followed every twist and curve the mountain had to offer. After looking at the map for a minute, Lyle asked me if I knew what this was? I told him other than a map of something going somewhere, that's about all I knew. Lyle then told me that it was a map that shows where the money that was taken from the South Dakota saving and loan was at. The money was buried in a steamer trunk that had over $30,000 in it.

I stood up and walked to the other side of the fire. I then asked Lyle, how he would know this?' That's when it all came out. "Because I was the banks manager, and staged the train hold up four years ago. I had four years until retirement and let's just say I put away money for retirement. But, Regan, I will need your help. I need you to help me with this map.' It was then I figured that it would be a good time to tell ole' Lyle about the cowboys that I also saw on this trail. He just stood there, white-faced as panic set in. After a few minutes, he told me that we had to bury the box somewhere that we could come back and get it in a few days. Grabbing a lantern we took the box, ink and paper. We counted off so many feet here and then there and all the time Lyle was drawing on this paper. We reached this really big rock that was sticking half out the ground. It kind of looked like an arrowhead. We marked off 102 chains and buried the box. Lyle said we would come back in the morning and see what the area looked like in the daylight. Then the strangest thing happened. Lyle handed me the necklace with the key. Then he said no one must get this key, no one, and that he could trust me to keep it safe till the time was right. We came back to camp and Lyle went to bed in his wagon and I pulled up another rock. The thunder was gone and it was another night were I would watch the stars dance, until I fell asleep.

In the morning the Fultons wanted to sleep in a little, so I went down to the creek to clean up and get water for breakfast. As soon as I bent over to wash my face, I heard the first of many gun shots. It sounded like canons firing in the hills, echoing all around me. I gathered up my sidearm and ran up the path to the campsite. Five men were standing around the wagons; some were still shooting. I drew my gun and fired into the men, striking one of them in the shoulder. They returned fire hitting me in the right leg. I fell to the ground and fired my last few shots. One of the men walked over to me and I recognized him. He was the sheriff I had talked to in Helena. "Well, well, well. What do we have here? I warned you boy about company you keep."

"What have you done?" I yelled at the men.

"What have I done? We haven't done anything, but it looks like you have. Killed all these people and wounded one of my deputies. You'll hang for this.' And with that the men dragged the dead bodies of the Fulton family and piled them up next to the camp fire. There was blood everywhere. The wagons were shot full of holes. I turned away and the men started to tear apart the wagons looking for something. It was then the sheriff walked over and kicked me in the face and asked me where the box was. Blood ran from my mouth and nose. I looked at my leg; it was grazed. I would be o.k. I told the sheriff I had no idea what he was talking about and then he started to hit and kick me. I blacked out. When I awoke the men had placed the Fultons bodies into the wagons and set the wagons on fire. They tied my hands behind my back and took my gun.

We rode almost none stop until we got back here to Helena. I was tried and convicted on the words of the sheriff and his men. And so here I am.

Thomas looked at his watch again. 6:00am. The sun was just starting to light up the town. Regan was now looking out of the little window. Thomas didn't know what to say; it had been quite a story. Thomas started, "Well Regan that was quite a story. Very detailed and it ran through smooth. I won't think that it will take much editing."

"Listen you have to do me a favor." Regan asked. "yes sure. What is it you need?" Thomas stuttered. "First, you have to believe that this is what happened. Second, I don't have anyone to give my stuff to and I'd like for you to have it. It's not much, but it's all I have." Regan stated.

Just then the locks on Regan's door turned and the old wooden door to the cell opened. Regan stood up and two men with weapons drawn rushed the room. The guard walked into the room and told Regan that it was time. Regan told the men that I would be taking all of his property and he didn't want anyone to watch his hanging. As they led Regan from the cell our eyes locked and his last words to me were, "You must believe me and write the truth."

I gathered my papers and followed Regan down the stone hall. They took him into a large room that veered off to the right of the hall. The door closed and I waited. I don't know what I was waiting for. I really just wanted to leave and get this over with. Then I heard a loud wooden creak, followed by a gurgling sound. A few minutes later a large thump, then a dragging sound. The door opened and the main guard told me to follow him to the office. Once there I was handed a large bag containing Regan's property. I was hurried out the back door and onto the street. I leaned against a street lamp. I took off my glasses and just stared off. The city was coming alive and a man just died and no one could care less.

I gathered myself and started to walk toward my rooms. I climbed the stairs, opened the door and collapsed on the bed. I was awoken by my landlord (Ike), who thought that I was dead. I assured him that I was just really tired. Looking at the clock it was 3:15 in the afternoon. I had slept over 8 hours. I closed my door, turned around and saw that sitting right in front of me was Regan's bag. I placed the bag on my bed and turned it upside down. It contained nothing special; just a pile of junk I thought. I collected the pictures, letters and clothes and placed them in a pile. I picked up Regan's cowboy hat and was going to place it on my desktop, when I noticed that for a hat it was really heavy. I took the hat over to the window and started to examine it. I noticed that there seemed to be something in the rim of the hat on the inside. I folded back the rim and first a few gold coins fell and then the end of a piece of leather cord fell out. I pulled on the cord and out came a key. It was the key on a necklace. I dropped the key and walked backward and fell onto the bed. I couldn't take my eyes off of the key. Just then I heard a knock at the door. I picked up everything and shoved the stuff back in the bag, placing the key in my pocket. When I opened the door, standing before me was the local sheriff.

"The boys at the jail said that Regan wanted you to have his property (laughing when he said it) so you might as well have this." The sheriff said. And with that he handed me a lance. "That should take care of that. Now you have yourself a good night." And then he was gone. I closed the door and looked at the lance. I thought to myself this must be the life spear. It was about then that I started to question everything. Had Regan told the truth? I unpacked the bag again and in every crack and seam of clothes I found gold coins. After I had gone through everything there was over $200.00 in gold. I was in shock and every time I looked at anything of Regan's I was dumbfounded. I had no idea what to do. Should I tell someone else or should I just take the money and forget it? Should I go to Elkhorn Mountain and find the other money and set things straight?

Then it came to me; if all of this is true (I thought), then where is the map to the steel box. I had gone through everything. I dumped out the bag once more. What have I missed? Then leaning against the bed I saw Regan's boots. I took one and tore out the inside and nothing. Then I tore out the other one. On the inside, under the boot's bottom first layer, was a worn piece of paper. It was folded into a small square. I slowly unfolded the paper and there it was, right in front of me. It was the map that would lead me to the steel box. It was just like Regan had said.

Slowly I walked to the window and looked out upon the street below and I asked myself one simple question. "As a reporter what would be the right thing to do?"

That was simple; I would go to Elkhorn Mountain and find this steel box, find the money and clear Regan's name. It sounded simple enough. Thomas decided that he would plan out his journey in the morning, but for now he had a story to write. A story that would be his last for the Montana Star.

Chapter Two
Getting It All Together

Thomas awoke with a feeling that he was being watched. As he turned, he came face to face with Ike. Thomas jumped back and noticed that Ike was carrying a mirror.

"What the hell are you doing?" exclaimed Thomas.

"Well after yesterday when you were laying here half dead, I figured that I'd better check on you." Thomas looked pointedly at the mirror. "Oh, the mirror was to check if you were still breathing." Ike said.

"Well, thank you, I think. While you are here, I have some things I need to talk to you about," Thomas stated. Thomas stood up and crossed over to the window. "I will be going a trip to see some older relatives that aren't doing well. I will need to pay the rent for the next four months."

"Lets see four months…(Ike said with a slight smile) ah, looks like you owe me around $15.00 and another $3.00 for watching your room for you. $18.00 should take care of it," Ike stated.

With that Thomas crossed to his dresser and got his wallet out. He handed Ike $18.00. "My rent is paid till the end of the month, this advance will extend it four months from that day. I will leave a note saying that if I do not return a month after the due date that you may have everything in this room. That should pay for any inconvenience that you may have," Thomas smiled back.

Ike agreed and Thomas wrote out the letter for Ike, then Ike exited laughing and shaking his head.

Thomas took out another piece of paper and started to outline his plan.

Write Regan's story/ hand it in/ take leave of absence
Gather maps, horses, wagon and 2 men to help
Pick up food supplies
Start journey to Elkhorn

It all seemed so simple on paper, but getting this together was quite a chore.

Thomas took out his wallet and the gold coins from Regan. He took a count and thought, "In cash and coin I have $234.00 and I have another $125.00 in savings…$359. I just might have enough," he thought.

Thomas worked for several hours, packing, collecting and checking his plan. He placed some items into a large cloth bag and set it next to Regan's bag. He turned and looked around the room and noticed he had finished. As he walked to the dresser, Regan's hat fell off the top of the bag and landed on the floor. Thomas picked it up and placed it on his head. It was a little big but it wasn't in too bad of a shape. Thomas looked into the hat to see if he could adjust the hat to fit his head. It was then that he noticed a large crease that ran crooked downward through the top of the hat. It was a wear crease, but something about it looked familiar. Thomas stared at the crease for a few seconds and then it hit him. He jumped up and went through Regan's bag and found the boot containing the map. Digging out the map Thomas placed it next to the line in the hat. It was almost an exact match of the main line on the map. It made a curve almost where the big steel box was. Thomas had an idea.

He crossed over to where he kept his quill and inks. He dug through the ink, but couldn't find any brown. Black ink would show, but brown would match the hat. He thought to himself. Looking around the room, he saw laying on the floor with the stuff he had taken out of Regan's bag was a brown tobacco plug. He had never chewed tobacco before, but he would give it a try. Picking it up, he bit off an end-corner of the plug and sat at the table looking out the window. He chewed it like gum and started to get a little dizzy. Leaning over the table, he spit the tobacco into a small cup. Thomas was really getting light headed and he thought to himself, "Why would anyone chew this stuff?" It was about this time that Thomas stood up and ran down the hall from his room to the bathroom. A few minutes later Thomas returned to his room, sat down at the table again and looked into the cup. With his hands holding up his face, it dawned on him. "I could have just added water to the damn stuff and got the same effect." The liquid was brown and just a tad bit darker than the hat. Thomas turned the hat inside out. He placed the quill into the liquid and copied the map onto the top of the hat. After he was done he looked over his handy work. It looked good. But what about the numbers he thought. Taking off his belt, he wrote the numbers using just the quill. He cut into the leather belt writing down the numbers in order.

He waited, refolded the hat and tried it on. Still too big. Taking out needle and thread, Thomas puckered the inside of the hat and sewed the pucker, making the hat smaller. Looking into the mirror, he sat it on his head. "Better, much better."

He said out loud.

Thomas picked up the map, he looked it over for a moment. He then lit a match and held it to the paper, letting it burn up in his dry sink. He watched it burn looking deep into the flame, watching the colors turn from white to blue and then just ashes. He poured water into the sink and waited. He poured the water out the window and watched it run down the rain spout. As he was closing the window, Thomas noticed the sheriff and a few men looking up his way. Thomas waved, smiled and closed the window. As he looked to see who the men were, he noticed that one of them was Ike. "Strange," he thought. Thomas then turned and picked up his typewriter and set it on the table. He placed paper into the rollers, gathered up his notes and started writing Regan's story. It took over a week to write Regan's story. Thomas wrote and then rewrote. He had a large stack of papers wadded up and lying near the bed.

It was early morning on Friday, when Thomas finished and noticed that his stomach was growling very loudly. He realized then that he had not eaten in a very long time. He crossed to the dresser and cut off a slice of bread and cheese. He was done with the story, done with the newspaper; and, most of all, he was done with this town. "This town was like a bad dream" Thomas thought. He layed down on the bed and slept until the first light started to show through the window.

Thomas grabbed his hat and wallet and walked out the door. He exited the rental house and headed toward main street. His first stop would be the bank. He needed to change the gold coins for cash. Upon entering the bank, he dug deep into his pocket for the bag of gold coins. As Thomas got the gold out, his necklace with the key on it fell out. The bank teller just gave Thomas a weird stare.

"Is there anything wrong?" Thomas asked.

"It's your hat. It doesn't much match the suit that you are wearing," the teller stated.

"Oh this ole' thing' I'm changing my clothes later and I didn't want to forget it," Thomas explained.

Thomas placed the bag of gold onto the table. "I would like to exchange this for paper currency. I've been saving it for a while. And I would also like to withdraw all the money out of my savings account."

The teller took the bag and dumped out the gold and counted back the money in bills. She then went to get the bank manager to sign off on the cancelled account. She came back and handed Thomas the rest of his money. Thomas exited the bank with all eyes upon him. "I definitely need to change clothes," Thomas thought. He crossed the street to the hardware store and went inside. He selected a few pairs of pants, shirts and also a new pair of boots. He went into the changing room and came out a new man. Now his clothes matched his hat; they were new but they matched. He paid for everything and as he exited the store he threw his old clothes in the wooden barrel, sitting in front of him. Carrying his bags, he walked down to the stockyard and started to look around. He asked the stableman if he knew where he could get a good wagon and a team of horses. The stableman sent him down to the Carter's house.

"It's the big green house on the left with the white barn. Can't miss it," the stableman said. Thomas thanked the man and walked to the Carter's house. As he approached the house, he noticed some nice looking horses running along the fence line. An older man, with his foot on the fence chewing on a piece of straw, looked over toward Thomas.

"What is it you need, boy?" the man asked.

"I'm looking for a good wagon and a few horses. Are there any for sale here?" asked Thomas.

"You'll have to talk to Ms. Carter. She is in the main house," the man said.

Thomas turned and walked down the rock covered path to the house. He knocked on the door and he heard a woman laughing as she approached the door.

"Yes, may I help you?" she asked.

"Yes, I'm Thomas Bach and I am looking to buy a wagon and a team of pulling horses. Do you have any for sale? The stableman said that you might," Thomas explained.

"Why, yes, we do. How much are you looking to spend?" she said as she looked at his new clothes and old hat.

"I don't have much," Thomas said.

"Well, let me show you what I have. By the way, I'm Ms. Carter.

And with that she took Thomas along the side of the porch and down to the white barn. Someone was in the barn. It looked like a woman from the back. She was wearing jeans, boots and a short sleeve shirt. She had her long brown hair tied back with a black string.

"Nancy this is Thomas. He's looking to buy a wagon and a team of horses. Go fetch that older pair in stall number three," Miss Cater asked.

"Yes, Ms. Carter," Nancy said as she went to get the horses.

"A far as a wagon, I have only one for sale. I just had new bearings, wheels and harness straps put on. She doesn't look that good, but she'll hold up on the trail." Ms. Cater explained as Nancy came bringing up two very large horses.

"These are draft horses. They will pull anything and I'll give you a deal on the whole lot. By the way where are you headed?" Ms, Carter asked.

"I'm headed to see some older relatives that I haven't seen in a while. Up to Elkhorn Mountain."

Nancy looked at Thomas and smiled. "Have you ever been to Elkhorn Mountain Mr…?"

"Bach, Thomas Bach. No I haven't, but I'm sure it's lovely this time of year. It being late spring and all," Thomas said.

"I lived only a day's ride from that mountain, a place called Chester. I really miss that town and that mountain," Nancy said.

"Okay, Mr. Bach, you can chat on you own time," Ms Carter started up. "I figure for the wagon, horses and extra parts that it will come to $175.00 plus I am not guaranteeing anything. All you get is a sales receipt. If you want a guarantee, that will cost you $250.00"

"Well that sounds like a deal I guess. What do you think Nancy?" Thomas asked.

Nancy smiled and said, "Well, these horses are in good shape and can pull. If you're not looking for anything fancy in a wagon this one is sound enough."

"Well, it's a deal." Thomas said and handed over the money.

"I still have some stops yet to make, but I'll be back in three hours to pick up my wagon and horses. Please have them ready to leave tonight."

"I'll put Nancy right on it and it will be ready by then. Nice doing business with you Mr. Bach." Ms. Carter said as she walked out of the barn.

"Are you really going to Elkhorn Mountain, Mr. Bach?" Nancy asked.

"Please call me Thomas and yes, I was hoping to leave tonight before dark."

"Well I'll have the team ready to go in three hours.' Nancy smiled.

With that Thomas tipped his hat to her and off he went up the path from the barn to the main street. "That wasn't too bad of a deal." He thought to himself. Then it dawned on to him that he never saw the wagon. But he thought that Nancy and Ms. Carter wouldn't try to pull one over on him. Thomas hoped he was right.

Thomas then took out his list. The newspaper office was next. As he walked to the newspaper his packages were getting heavy. He came to the building and started to climb the long staircase to the main press room and his office. Once in his office, he laid down his packages and walked to his editor office. As he walked into the room everyone just looked at him and some even laughed. One person yelled, "Look, it's cowboy Bach." Thomas just kept walking until he reached the editor's, Bob Smith's, office. Thomas knocked and he heard the invitation to come in. He opened the door and went in.

"What in the name of heaven have you done to your self Thomas?" Smith asked.

"I'm changing a few things in my life right now. The way I dress is just one of them" Thomas said and he handed Mr. Smith the story on Regan Paul Wright.

"What the hell is this? Oh, I see it's the Regan story. What a cruel man he was. You know they buried him up on Cheater Hill. Kind a fits him, doesn't it?" Smith said.

"Well about my payment for this story. I'd like to get paid in cash this time." Thomas said.

"Cash. What's wrong with a check?" Smith asked.

"I need to leave Helena and go to visit some relatives that are not doing well. Some may not be alive by the time I reach them. I will also need a leave of absence, for four months. I have just recently got this message, but I wanted to finish the story on Regan before I left. I hope you understand Mr. Smith." Thomas said.

"Oh well, family and all. I guess we could do without you for a short time." Smith then yelled for his secretary. She entered and Smith told her to get the cash box. She returned with it and handed it to Mr. Smith.

"Let's see you had one major story and a few small ones. I shouldn't do this without looking over what you wrote, but here's what I think I owe you." and with that Smith handed Thomas $43.00.

"Thank you, Mr. Smith, and I'll be returning in four months."

And then Thomas exited the office with a smile on his face. He knew the story that he wrote about Regan was good and it told the true facts. But Thomas had not wrote about some of the things. Things like the key around his neck or the steel box or even the money for that matter. It was just the cut and dried story of an honest man. A story he was sure Mr. Smith would rewrite anyway.

Thomas gathered up his packages and climbed down the long steps to the main street. The town was busy now. People and wagons were everywhere. Thomas looked at his list. He would pick up food and supplies on the way out of town. The last item he needed to fill was men. He needed to hire at least 1 man to help him. Carrying his packages Thomas crossed the street to the saloon. He ordered a beer and a meal. When the barkeep came with his meal, Thomas asked. "Do you know any men that I can hire to go on a trip I need to go on."

"Not really, no one in here. But you may want to try the gentleman at the end of the bar. He said something last week about leaving Helena," the barkeep said.

Thomas picked up his meal and drink and crossed to the end of the bar. Surely the barkeep was mistaken. This man was old, fat and drunk. But Thomas starting talking to the man. "Excuse me, sir. The barkeep said that you may want a job."

The man looked up at Thomas. He was older than Thomas thought. The man stood up and said. "Why, yes, I would." He cocked his head to the right, "What do you need done?" he asked.

"I'm going on a trip to see relatives and I would be needing help with the journey—Cooking and tending to the horses. Just a general handyman," Thomas explained.

"The name is Jake. Jake Morgan. And I'm the best damn cook around and as far as horses go there isn't one I can't ride. As far as Indians go I can shot the eye out of a gold dollar coin from ten yards" Jake Said laughing.

"Mr. Morgan."

"Call me Jake, everyone does."

"O.k. Jake, do you mind if I ask how old you are" Thomas inquired.

"That's a fair question. I'm 58 year young. Yep born on a leap year. That's why I'm so spry. I could tell you stories about me winning shootin' contests and about my four wives, but I'll save'em for the trail. Now, what are you paying?" Jakes asked.

"Well, Jake, what is it that you require as payment for this trip?" Thomas asked.

"Well, I'll need two cases of whiskey and $2.00 a day," Jake said.

"How about 3 cases of whiskey and .50 a day?" Thomas suggested.

"You have got your self a deal. When do I start?" Jake said. "Where are you headed?"

"We are headed for Elkhorn Mountain. I'm going to visit family on the other side of Elkhorn. I will need you till I get the base of the mountain." Thomas explained.

"Elkhorn? Who in their right mind would want to go to that God forsaken place? If not for the snakes, bears and mountain lions that would kill ya, the Crow would damn sure do it," Jake Stated.

"That's fine. You don't have to go, but that's the deal. Right now I want you to go and pick out our supplies at Kennedy's mercantile. I'll pick up the wagon and I'll meet you there in one hour. We will be gone for at least 90 days, so get everything that you'll need," Thomas ordered.

"Will do. Met you in one hour at Kennedy's. I'll be ready. I'll pick up some odds and ends for the trip," Jake said.

With that, Thomas shook Jakes hand and then finished his meal and beer. Thomas left the saloon carrying his packages and headed to the Carter's. As Thomas walked he thought that he should only need one man. Jake said he was a sure shot and great cook. And with the skills that Thomas had he was sure that this was all he would need. Jake's drinking was also an added bonus. Thomas would supply the whiskey once they reach the final location as that Jake's head would be clear for the trip, but he would be drunk where Thomas finally located the box and money. This might just work out. Thomas crossed over to Ms. Carter's place and headed to the barn. "Maybe I'll see Nancy again before I go," Thomas hoped. As he entered the barn, Ms. Carter came from behind the wagon and walked to Thomas.

"Here you go Mr. Bach. Ready to go," Carter said.

Thomas looked at the horses. They seemed out of place. The wagon was all right, but the horses were twice the size of the wagon. Since he had already paid for them, there was no turning back now. The wagon had a nice cover over it. It looked new and, like Ms. Carter had said, new wheels and bearings.

"Where's Nancy?" Thomas asked.

"Oh, she's around here somewhere. Have you ever driven a team before Mr. Bach?" Ms. Carter asked.

"It's been a while, but I think I can remember how." Thomas stretched the truth. He had been six years old the last time he drove one and his father had helped him.

Thomas climbed into the wagon and picked up the reins. He gave a little slap on the horses' backs and slowly, very slowly, they walked out of the barn. Thomas crossed up the hill toward main street to pick up Jake. He slapped the reins again and yelled go, but the horses still just crawled with the wagon through the main street. He reached

Kennedy's and saw Jake was standing next to a pile of wooden boxes.

"Do you have everything that you'll need, Jake?" Thomas asked.

"I sure do, Mr. Bach," Jake answered.

Thomas went into the store to pay for the supplies.

"I'll need to review and pay for the supplies that are under the name Thomas Bach." He stated to the storekeep as he approached.

"Lets see. This total is $86.35," The storekeep stated.

Thomas just looked at the man. "Let me see that bill," Thomas asked.

He read the list out loud:

50 lbs flour

20 lbs bacon strap

50 lbs dried beans

8 cases of Rose Whiskey

Thomas stopped right there, "We need to change this to 2 not 8 cases."

The grocer yelled at one of his boys and he went outside to get the 6 other cases. The boy returned with Jake.

"Listen, Mr. Bach. I've changed my mind about the pay. I'd like to be paid in whiskey, not money, and those 8 cases will fill the bill," Jake stated.

Thomas looked at Jake and said, "Fine, but, I will warn you right now, if things don't work out between us, I will not hesitate to break every bottle." Thomas leaned forward and looked into Jake's eye's. "Every bottle, do I make myself clear? I will dole out the bottles and you will not be drunk on the job!"

"Yes, Mr. Bach."

The rest of the list looked good, so Thomas paid the man and walked to the wagon. Two boys and Jake were laughing as they loaded the last of the boxes onto the wagon. Thomas climbed up and Jake sat at his side. Thomas slapped the reins and yelled let's go! The horses again slowly pulled away from the store. Jake had a grin on his face and kept looking at Thomas. Thomas just kept looking forward.

He knew he had one last stop. He had to go to his room and get the last of his things. They pulled up and parked in front of the boarding house.

"I'll just be a minute," Thomas told Jake.

He approached his room and noticed that the door was ajar. Slowly, he pushed open the door to reveal his room. It was in shambles. Someone had torn apart his place. Things were everywhere. Thomas just stood looking. He saw bags of clothes and Regan's things lying strewn across his bed. He started to pick up what ever he thought that he might need. He grabbed the spear and headed down he hallway yelling.

"Ike! Ike! Where the hell are you Ike!"

Slowly a door opened up and Ike appeared.

"What is it you want, Bach?" Ike asked.

"My room-My room is torn up. What is the meaning of this?"

"All I know is that sheriff McKenzie and a few boys stopped by and wanted to see your room. The next thing I knew it looked like that. I figured that you had left already and I had four months to get it back in order. It'll be fixed by the time you get back. Don't worry." Ike said.

"It had damn well better be!" And with that Thomas carried out his stuff and threw it in the back of the wagon.

"Not much of a packer are you? Just grab and go," laughed Jake.

"Jake, did we pack enough ammo?" Thomas asked.

"We got two rifles and two colt 45's. and enough ammo to hold off a small army," Jake said.

"Good, we may just need it."

Then with a slap of the reins and a deeper voice, Thomas made the horses move a little faster than before. Thomas looked at his watch. It was 2:35 in the afternoon; they would have a good four hours until pitching camp for the night. As the wagon traveled through the last of Helena, Thomas made a hard left. Jake nearly fell off the wagon and Thomas heard a strange noise.

"Where are you going Mr. Bach? Elkhorn is the other way." Questioned Jake.

"I know but I have one last stop," Thomas explained.

The big draft horses now earned their keep as they pulled up Cheater's Hill. Regan's grave wasn't hard to find. The dirt on top was fresh and a white paper with Regan's name was on it. Thomas climbed off the wagon and walked to the grave. He took off his hat and looked down at the fresh dirt.

"Well, I think everything is ready. I handed in your story. I wrote the truth Regan. It will be up to them if they want to rewrite it or not. I hope everything is true and I am as ready as I'll ever be. I think I know what to do with the money when I get it. Hey, I'm wearing your hat; it'll be like you're riding with us. Take care Regan and I'm sure I'll see you someday. I just hope it not too soon." With that Thomas smiled and hopped back up onto the wagon.

The wagon slowly rolled down Cheater's Hill and back to the main road. As the last of Helena was disappearing behind Thomas and Jake, Thomas stood up and yelled, "Goodbye Helena! May I never see you again," And with that Thomas slapped the reins and the horses and sped up a little, leaving a slight cloud behind the wagon. Thomas then grabbed the key through his shirt and held on to it as he drove along the trail.

Chapter Three
The Journey to Elkhorn

Jake and I followed the dirt road out of Helena and watched the sunset start to set to the right of us. I turned to Jake and said, "I guess we had better set up camp, before it gets to dark out to see."

"Sounds like a plan to me," Jake said.

Just then a voice called out from the wagon, "yep that sure does sound like a plan."

Thomas stopped the wagon and handed the reins to a laughing Jake. Thomas climbed over the seat, uncovered the wagon and there she was. She was just sitting on a wooden box looking and smiling at Thomas.

"Everyone. Out of the wagon, NOW!" Thomas yelled.

Jake jumped off the wagon and Nancy climbed out of the back. She stood next to Jake while Thomas stood speechless.

"Before you go crazy, Mr. Bach, let me explain. I worked for Ms. Carter for years with the understanding of getting a piece of land. She told me last week that she had no money left to give me and she wouldn't give me the land. She was getting ready to sell everything off.

I just wanted a ride to Chester. Please, Mr. Bach, just let me ride that far. I have no money nor do I have any family left," Nancy explained.

Thomas turned and looked at the sunset. Nancy came over and placed her hand on his shoulder.

"What's it going to hurt Mr. Bach? She is already here. What are you going to do? Turn her out to the wild?" Jake asked.

Thomas shifted the dirt with his boots. Looking up to both of them he said. "First of all, you can stop calling me Mr. Bach. Call me Thomas or Tom, if you like. Yes, you can ride as far as Chester, but you will have to pull your own weight. Is that clear?"

"Well, I did bring my guns with me and I'll hunt for supper," Nancy said.

"Sounds good to me. I'll start a fire and setup camp." Jake said.

Nancy walked off into the woods and Thomas watched her enter a clearing.

"I'll get some wood," Thomas said.

Thomas kept Nancy in site as he walked to the woods' edge. Nancy quickly raised up her rifle and fired. Thomas waited to see what would happen next. He thought that she was really a handsome looking woman. He liked her long brown hair, but she was a little thin. He wondered just how old she was.

Nancy crossed over and picked up the rabbit she had shot and took out the knife she kept in her boot. She started to gut and skin the rabbit. As she stood up, she noticed movement in the woods. She placed the rabbit in a little bag and crossed back over into the forest. Nancy walked quietly through the trees and bushes.

Meanwhile Thomas walked to the edge of the treeline, but couldn't see Nancy anymore. He thought that maybe she had crossed back and was at camp with supper. As he turned, he heard something snap, like a twig or a branch. Thomas stopped in his tracks and crouched down on his knees.

Nancy got close to the person. She could see that he was low to the ground. She picked up a rock and threw it on the opposite side of her. The person stood and started to run. Nancy jumped through the brush and wrestled the person to the ground. She pinned him down and came face to face, with Thomas.

"Well this is kinda awkward," Thomas said.

Nancy got off of Thomas. "I'm so sorry! I didn't know it was you." She got this mad look on her face. "Why were you spying on me? You need to explain yourself, Mr. Bach!"

"I didn't want you out here by yourself. This is really mean country. Anything can happen. It's best to have someone with you at all times. Besides, I was gathering wood for the fire," Thomas explained.

"Oh, so where is the wood?" Nancy asked.

"I never got that far," Thomas said as he got up.

Thomas held out his hand and pulled Nancy up.

"We had better get back to camp before Jake starts drinking. We'll get this rabbit of yours in the pot," Thomas said smiling.

Thomas and Nancy walked into the camp where Jake had built a big fire and had the water hot and rolling. Nancy handed the rabbit to Jake. "I kill and you cook."

"I wouldn't argue with that. Where's the extra wood?" Jake said laughing.

"Still in the woods," Thomas replied.

The three ate supper and Thomas took his bag and leaned it against a large rock sticking out of the ground. He looked up at the stars and thought about Regan. He watched the stars in the sky. They were so bright shining down. The moon was almost full. All of the sudden Thomas heard someone playing a harmonica. Thomas turned and saw Jake sitting by the fire with Nancy, playing a slow tune. Thomas laid his hat beside his hip and fell asleep to the sounds of the night and the music.

Thomas awoke early in the morning to crying. He looked at his watch. 2:30. As Thomas approached the wagon, he could tell Nancy was sobbing. Slowly Thomas walked up to the side of the wagon.

"I'm sorry if I woke you," Nancy said still crying. "But this part of the country brings back bad memories." Then Nancy stepped out of the wagon and stood next to Thomas.

"It was bad when the Crow came. I was sleeping in the barn, because we had a horse that was having trouble birthing. I was woke up by to the sounds of people screaming. Indians were everywhere and my family was either being shot or burned alive. I panicked and hid beneath a trap door leading to a crawlspace under the barn. I crawled to the end of the space and watched the Crow leave town with everything. Horses, food, cattle...just everything. I guess I passed out or fell asleep, but when I woke in the morning, there were only three of us left. Everyone else was either dead or taken prisoner. We walked to the next town and they came and buried the dead and helped the three of us survivors settle in at Helena. That's when I met Ms. Carter," Nancy wiped her eyes with her sleeve and looked up at Thomas. O.k. now that I look like a fool."

Thomas took Nancy and held her close and said. "I can't imagine what you went through. No one can understand that. But you need to look ahead. You need to think of the future," Thomas said.

"That's easy for you to say. That's easy for anyone to say." Nancy said as she turned around.

Thomas came up behind her and wrapped his arms around her. He pulled her close and looked up at the stars. "Look at those stars. They are there for only one purpose; they shine and sometimes if you look really close they race across the sky." Nancy looked up at the sky. "Nancy, they have a place to go just like all people. Their paths intertwine with each other and some even die," Thomas said.

Just then two stars streaked across the sky. "Quick! Make a wish!" Thomas said. They each watched as the stars faded into the dark. Nancy turned and came face to face with Thomas. They closed their eyes and their lips met. Thomas couldn't remember feeling like this. They kissed and finally broke apart. Nancy looked down. "You must think I'm a terrible person. We hardly know each other and here we are kissing under the stars," Nancy said.

"No, on the contrary, I think you are a wonderful person. The kind of person I'd like to know better. We can go slowly. Who knows; maybe it was just the night air that drew us together. Or maybe it was...," that was all Thomas could say. Nancy stretched up and said, "Oh, shut up and kiss me!" and with that they sat down by the wagon holding each other and looking into the night. They watched the sun start to rise and then Jake stumbled out of the front of the wagon and hit the ground right in front of them.

"Morning, Jake." Nancy and Thomas said as he straightened himself up. With his hands on his sides, Jake looked at the sunrise and then at Thomas and Nancy. "Well, I'll be," Jake mumbled.

Thomas stood up and held out his hand to Nancy and kissed her as she stood up. They walked hand in hand to the front of the wagon. Thomas noticed a broken whiskey bottle lying in the dirt.

"Jake," Thomas said.

"Yes, Mr. Bach," Jake answered.

"From now on we are not to break any bottles or any type of glass. When you have emptied your bottles, I want the labels torn off and replaced with water. Is that understood?" Thomas ordered.

"Yes, Mr. Bach. It won't happen again," Jake said.

"Now, let's pack up while we get breakfast and be on our way," Thomas said.

The three of them packed and Nancy started breakfast. By the time Jake and Thomas had almost everything packed breakfast was on. Nancy had made creamed bacon over bread. The three ate the fine meal and Thomas kept looking at Nancy. She would just smile and give him a devilish look back. When they were done, they finished loading the wagon.

"Oh, Jake, I think that Nancy will be riding up front with me today. You can take up a spot in the back of the wagon." Thomas said. Everyone climbed aboard and Jake started to complain right away.

"You know it would be more comfortable back here if you get rid of this damn spear," Jake yelled.

"Hand me the spear," Thomas said.

Thomas took the spear and placed it into the crack in the wood between the front seat and the wagon. It stuck out at an angle. Thomas slapped the reins and the team moved forward. As they rode down the dirt road Nancy was full of questions for Thomas.

"So, Mr. Bach, where are you from?" Nancy asked as she hugged his arm.

"I was an orphan. I didn't really know my parents. I was raised in an orphanage in Virginia," Thomas said.

"That's terrible," Nancy said.

"Oh, it wasn't that bad. When I was 9, I was adopted by this nice family from Richmond. They had a large plantation and worked from sunrise to sunset. I didn't get to do hard work till summer time. Instead, I would be tutored by my set of teachers. I had one for the Math and Sciences and another that taught me English and Music. And when I was 19, I enrolled in a college for writing. I graduated and took a job with the Montana Star. My adopted family fought over the farm when mother died. My adopted father didn't like me anyway. So, I never went back," Thomas ended.

Nancy just looked at him, her eyes fill with torment. She was thinking to herself, "He's not much different than me."

"Thomas we have each other now, that's the important thing," Nancy said.

"Can I tell you a secret?" Thomas asked.

"Sure. If we are going to be together, we shouldn't keep secrets from one another. What is it?" Nancy asked.

"I had a crush on you the moment I saw you standing in Ms. Carter's barn," Thomas looked at Nancy. "Just the way you were standing there, with that smile on you face. I thought I must be dreaming," And with that Thomas leaned over and kissed her, dropping the reins to his feet and holding her face. "I hope this last's Nancy. I just hope that you don't find me boring and leave," Thomas ended and grabbed up the reins.

"Oh, I am pretty sure that you will have to leave without me. For now you're stuck with me. Like it or not," Nancy stated.

They had been going down the road for about 4 hours. Then finally, in the distance, they could see Elkhorn Mountain. "Still about a day's ride, but we should be there by tomorrow this time," Thomas said looking at his watch.

"11:20. In another hour we'll stop, rest and water the horses."

Jake spoke up, "It's about time. The Wolly river should be close. Should be able to hear it in a few minutes."

Sure enough, in about 15 minutes they could hear the sounds of the river. Thomas pulled the wagon around a bend and came to a clearing. He jumped down and helped Nancy from her seat. They walked hand in hand to the rear of the wagon and helped Jake out of the back.

"This would make a great spot for the night, Thomas. Let's just camp here and get an early start in the morning,." Nancy said.

"What do you think Jake? You like this spot? Or should we move on?" Thomas questioned.

"It looks good. I'll start with the horses and then unpack the wagon," Jake said.

Thomas had started gathered kindling for the fire when he heard this strange sound coming from the road. "It sounds like metal hitting each other," He thought. As he walked to the edge of the woods, he saw what was making the noise. It was a large covered wagon about twice the size of his. It had pots and pans hanging from the side and they were hitting each other as the wagon went over every bump in the road. He saw Nancy and Jake start to walk up to the wagon. The driver, a big burly man, pulled back hard on the reins. Thomas caught up with the wagon and stood beside Nancy.

"Well, you sure do make a lot of noise. Welcome to our camp. I'm Thomas Bach."

The big man leaned over the side of his wagon and spit a long string of tobacco and it hit the ground at Jake's feet.

"People call me Mole. My real name if Moe Stevens, but you can call me Mole. I sell town to town. Anything and everything that you could possibly need I have on this wagon," Mole said.

"This is Nancy and this is Jake, and you are welcome to spend the night if you like," Thomas added.

"That sounds mighty nice of you folks. I think I'll take you up on that offer. I've been riding day and night trying to put some miles between me and those damn Indians. Ran into them back by Gulch Creek. It was not a good business transaction," Moe said.

"Well, at least you're still alive. Come on down and pull up a seat, ole timer," Jake said.

So everyone went back to doing what they had been doing before Mole pulled in. Thomas gathered wood, Nancy got the cooking pots out and Jake just mostly talked to Mole. They got the fire going and set the pots over the fire. Thomas poured the last of the water into the pot and Jake placed potatoes and dried meat into it. While the pot was cooking Jake and Mole sat around still talking and Thomas and Nancy went to gather water.

When they found the river, they also found tracks in the mud bank. Thomas studied the tracks but couldn't decide who or what they were until he found, bare feet running along the edge of the river. Thomas and Nancy followed the tracks. They came upon the death smell of a half rotten deer. The tracks lead straight to the carcass.

"Looks like Indians killed this deer and left half of it. It doesn't make much sense. Why only half a deer? You can see cut marks into the meat and then nothing." Thomas said.

"Thomas," Nancy said slowly and in a low voice.

"What a waste, you could..." Thomas was interrupted by Nancy who was a little more stern this time, "Thomas! I want you to stand up and walk slowly back to me."

"What?" Thomas said.

"If you want to live, move slowly and keep looking down. But move!" Nancy hissed.

Thomas backed away from the deer and slowly came to where

Nancy stood. He looked up he came face to face with a large grizzly bear that was standing about 30 feet on the other side of the deer. Thomas grabbed Nancy and started running as fast as they could along the river. The Grizzly caught their scent and took off at a full charge chasing them. They started to climb the hill to the camp when the bear caught up with them. Thomas grabbed a tree limb and hit the bear with it, only to have it break into and fall to his feet. Nancy grabbed Thomas and they climbed the hill. As they reached the top Thomas fell and Nancy yelled. "Help! Help! Thomas is going to be killed! Jake... Mole!"

Nancy held onto Thomas's shirt and pulled him up. Just then two gun shots were heard and the bear fell backward down the hill. Jake and Mole were standing there with their guns smoking looking down the hill. The bear didn't move as they started down to the bottom of the hill. The large bear lay motionless next to the water.

"Thomas, are you alright?" Nancy asked as she hugged him.

"It's my ankle. I think the bear scratched it," Thomas said.

Nancy took off his boot and pulled open his pant leg. There was a large cut about 6 inches long and 1/4 inch deep.

"How's it look?" Thomas asked.

"Just lay down. Jake I need water, cloth and some kind of medicine," Nancy commanded.

"We got water and I can make a cloths wrap, but we don't have any medicine," explained Jake.

"Hey Mole, you got any medicine in that wagon of yours?" Jake yelled.

"Yes, I sure do. I get it," Moe answered.

Nancy grabbed Thomas and hugged him close. "I can't believe what happened. You could have died. I could have lost you," Nancy said crying.

"It's okay, I feel fine. We are both alive and well. Now stop crying and help me up." Thomas said.

"Here, this should help. We are going to have to stitch this cut up.

It's bleeding really badly, but that's a good thing. Jake, do you have any whiskey? Mole said.

"I might have a bottle or two laying around," Jake said looking at Thomas.

Nancy got Thomas to stand up and they made it to the wagon. She sat him down and smiled at him. Jake handed Mole a bottle.

"This is gonna to sting a little. Someone might want to hold him down," Mole said.

Mole poured the whiskey over the cut. Thomas let out a scream and Nancy held him down. Mole turned around and placed Thomas's leg between his and sat down. He took his needle and thread and sewed up the cut. Pouring whiskey over the cut after every stitch. Thomas settled down when Mole was done and he handed Nancy the medicine.

"I'll put this on and place the wrap on," Nancy said.

Jake and Mole walked over the hill to where the bear lay dead. It was then that Mole noticed the tracks.

"Look here Jake," Mole said. "Indian tracks."

"How fresh are they?" Jake asked.

"Looks like maybe a week," Mole said.

"This bear must be at least 600 pounds. It would be a shame to just let the meat rot. Let's cut it up," Jake said.

Mole and Jake went back to the wagon to get the team of horses and a rope. Nancy and Thomas were sitting on the end of the wagon. Nancy was trying to place Thomas's boot back on his foot.

"We are going to drag the bear up over the hill and cut him up. Gonna be eating meat tonight," Jake laughed.

"I'd like to have the hide," Thomas said. "Do we have enough salt to start tanning it?

"I'll sell you some salt and don't forget you owe me $1.00 for the Medicine," Mole said to Thomas.

"Make up a bill for the supplies and I would also like to know what else you have on your wagon. I may want to go shopping, and get some things that we might need before you leave," Thomas said.

Thomas's leg was starting to thump and bleed through the bandage. He placed it up high, setting it on a case of whiskey. Nancy went to the river and loaded up some water. Mole and Jake took the horses to the edge of the hill and tied the rope around the bear and the horses drug the bear up the hill. Jake and Mole started to cut up the carcass.

"Here, you need to drink as much water as you can. You know if you would have just kept running, he wouldn't have got your leg. You shouldn't have stopped to hit him with that branch," Nancy said.

"I thought that he would get you. I thought..." Nancy stopped him.

"I know. When you turned and struck the bear, I saw the true man in you, Thomas. Someone that would risk his own life, to save another. You are a good man Thomas Bach. A man that I hope will not grow tired of me," Nancy then leaned down and kissed Thomas.

"Now I have to help get supper started. You just lay here and get better," Nancy said.

"Can you send Mole over here? I'll need to settle up with him," Thomas stated.

"Sure, but rest," Nancy replied.

Thomas watched as Nancy walked away, and for the first time in his life, he felt loved. She just had this way of making him feel special. He hoped that this wasn't just a trail romance. He hoped it would last.

"What do you need, Thomas?" Mole asked.

"Well, I need to do some shopping. Let's see... do you have other medicines in your wagon?" Thomas asked

"Sure," Mole said.

"Well, I don't have much money left, but I want you to come up with a medicine kit. Meds, bandages ointments, and whatever you think we might need. Also, do you have anything that a lady might like?" Thomas asked.

"I have an assortment of necklaces and lockets," Mole said.

"Bring them over and let me look at them but don't let Nancy see.

Thanks, Mole. Thanks for everything that you did today. And, by the way, nice shooting," Thomas ended.

"Well, to be honest, it was Jake that hit the bear in the head. He shot while on the dead run. I shot and hit the bear in the stomach. Jake is the one that killed it; he's the one you should be thanking," Mole said. "I'll get your stuff."

Thomas sat there and watched everyone working. Jake came over to the cook pot and tossed in cut up pieces of meat. Nancy brought up an arm load of wood and set it by the fire. Bending down, Thomas looked at his leg for the first time since it had been sewn up. The bleeding had stopped and it didn't really look that bad. He thought how different the whole bear attack could have went. Nancy and he could be dead or maybe just one of them. He promised himself that he would be really careful from here on out.

"How's this look?" Mole said, as he laid down a bag full of supplies. Moe stood there holding a cameo locket on an gold chain.

"How much for everything?" Thomas asked.

"Let see now... meds, bandages and necklace. Plus, I put you in some more ammo. You're looking at $17.00.

"I'll have to look and see if I have that much. Just put the stuff in back of our wagon and I'll get payment later. Let me see the necklace," Thomas asked.

Mole placed the necklace into Thomas's hands and walked away. Thomas looked at the Cameo, opened it up and looked inside. It was stamped 18k gold. He placed it into his shirt pocket and pulled out his wallet. He had some money hidden in the wagon, but he had at least $120 on him. He didn't have change. He had no single dollars left and he could only give Mole two tens. So, he yelled at Mole.

"Mole, come get your money"

"Had enough did ya?" Mole asked.

"Yes, but I'd also like to buy $3.00 worth of cast iron pans or just one large one. Here is $20.00." Thomas ended.

Moe took the money and returned with a large cast iron skillet, with a lid, and placed it into the wagon.

"That should bring us up to even," Moe said.

"Supper's on," yelled Nancy.

Everyone gathered around the fire, grabbed a plate and Nancy dipped out the stew. Thomas tasted the stew and, (other than the meat being tough) the gravy, potatoes, carrots and some cut up onions, tasted great.

"Nancy, this is really good. Where did you get onions out here?" questioned Thomas.

They're not onions. They're ramps. They're like an onion, but they pack a stink, if you don't cook them right," Nancy said.

"You can cook for me any day." Thomas stated.

Everyone agreed that the meal was great. After everyone had finished, Nancy cleaned up the dishes and Thomas sat with his leg up on a rock. Jake and Mole continued to cut up the bear. After Nancy got the cleaning done, she disappeared into the woods. After about 10 minutes, she reappeared carrying a arm full of branches. She layed then out and started to latch the end together in a box frame. Thomas watched her as she finished up. She had built a frame for the bear hide. She then crossed over to where Jake and Mole were and they pointed to where they had left the hide near the river bank.

Thomas stared at the sun, which was about 2 hours from setting. It was then he noticed dark clouds forming in the horizon. Nancy came up and over the hill carrying and dragging the hide. It was dripping wet. She had cleaned it in the river and made a cut up under its jaw. She had removed the brain, tongue and anything else, except the skull. Thomas watched her again as she stretched the bear across the frame and attached it. Then slowly she tied off the hide going from one corner, then to the opposite side corner. She did this until the hide was stretched taut on the frame, but not too tight. Thomas thought, "She must have done this before." Then she took the salt and began to rub it in, using a small rock. She worked almost an hour, and then leaned the hide against a tree.

As the sun was getting ready to set she came up to Thomas.

"How are you feeling, Thomas?" she asked.

"Oh, better. My leg has stopped swelling. I think I am going to take my boot off for the night, wash it out and let it breath over night," Thomas said.

"You know what, Thomas?" she asked as she kissed his cheek.

"What?" he asked.

"I really stink like bear. I'm going down to the river and take a much need bath." Nancy leaned down and looked into Thomas eyes and said. "Now Mr. Bach, don't follow me and no spying on me either." She kissed him and shot him a wink as she left to go to the wagon and to get fresh clothes. Thomas watched as she walked to the woods, turned and looked back at him, before entering the woods.

Then Jake and Mole came walking by Thomas carrying a large canvas tarp filled with meat. They headed up to Mole's wagon and started to pack the meat into wooden tubs. Thomas stood up and hobbled over to where Nancy had entered the woods. "Don't be following me, Mr. Bach," Thomas could hear her yell back. He looked back at Jake and Mole. They were too busy dealing with the meat to worry about him. Thomas slowly walked from the clearing. Down into the woods, he crossed to an area at the river bank, took off his boots and shirt and rolled up his pant legs. He waded into the water up to his knees. He could feel the cool water against his cut. He wanted the water to seep into it and take the last of the swelling down. He was standing there when suddenly he heard the splashing of water. "That must be Nancy," he thought. He walked around the bend in the river and peered through a bush. It was Nancy alright; she had her back toward him. She was sitting in a shallow pool bathing herself. She was humming a tune to as she bathed. Slowly, Thomas walked backward and went back to where he had left his clothes and boots. He didn't want to do anything stupid to mess up his relationship with Nancy. He put his socks and boots back on and carried his shirt over his shoulder. He climbed back up the hill and waited for Nancy.

After a few minutes Nancy came over the hill, carrying her old dirty clothes under her arm. She met Thomas and put her arms around him and kissed his check.

"I waited for you. Where were you?" she asked.

"I went and soaked my leg in the river," he said.

"Did you see anything you liked, while you were soaking?" Nancy asked.

"I saw you bathing in a shallow pool. I saw the sunset that gave a red hue to the water," Thomas paused "But like I said I'd like to take it slow and to answer you question, yes, I did see something that I'd like," He said smiling at Nancy. Thomas then leaned down and kissed her, drawing her near to him.

"What's this" Nancy asked.

"What are you talking about?" He replied.

Thomas had forgotten that he had no shirt on. His necklace hung down with the key fully exposed.

"Oh, that. Just a key I'm saving," He said.

"What does it go to?" She questioned.

"Well, it goes to a special box. I'll explain later, He said.

Just then as the last of the sun was going behind the mountain, a loud clap of thunder filled the air.

"We'd better take cover, looks like a storm is moving in. Jake, Mole get the horses bedded down and make sure the ropes are tight." Thomas and Nancy took extra rope and tied down the wagon. They pounded big wooden stakes into the ground and then tied the rope to it. Thomas and Nancy climbed into the wagon, just as Mole and Jake climbed into Mole's wagon. They pulled the canvasses down tight and waited for the storm.

Once inside, Thomas started to move the crates around to make room. He moved everything to the front and Nancy made a bed out of the rest of the wagon floor. He layed down on the blankets with Nancy as the rain started and the lightning lit up the sky. Thomas was worrying about the horses and Nancy was thinking about the storm.

It was at this time that Jake yelled over to Thomas, "Hey, Thomas, can you lay out a few bottles of whiskey in front of your wagon? I'll get them tonight after the storm." Jake said.

"Sure, Jake. I would hate to keep you from a hangover," Thomas replied.

Thomas snuggled down with Nancy and the wind caught up. As the rain came down in buckets and the wagon shook, the two held each other as the night wore on. He placed his arm around her and she rested her head on his chest. Then they all fell asleep, with the sounds of the storm.

Thomas awoke to the sound of Jake playing his harmonica. He gently rocked Nancy.

"Wake up sleepy head," He said as he looked at his watch. It's already 8:15. We need to get going if we are going to make it to Elkhorn by evening."

Nancy sat up and stretched, then turned and kissed Thomas.

"How are you feeling this morning? I slept great. Better than I have in years," she said.

Thomas sat up. "I'm feeling really good too. I want to check my leg. It's a little stiff. But I think it's okay.," he said.

"What is that noise? Sounds like a rooster is dying," Nancy laughed.

They both climbed out of the wagon and there sat Jake on a rock by the fire. Thomas looked around. Mole was gone.

"Morning Jake. Where's Mole?" Thomas asked.

"He left early this morning. He said that he had to get an early start to make it to Helena. He left you a present Miss. Nancy" Jake said.

Jake handed her the package. She grabbed it and handed it to Thomas.

"What is this?" He questioned.

"Open it silly. I bought you something that you need," Nancy said.

Thomas opened the box and inside it was a brand new hat. Kind of like his old one. He took his old one off and placed the gift on his head. It was a perfect fit.

Nancy picked up his old hat and said, "Now we can get rid of this old hat. It really doesn't fit you very well."

She tossed the hat into the bushes. Thomas ran and grabbed the hat. Jake and Nancy just looked at him.

"This new hat is great, but it's too nice for the trail. I'll wear my old one and leave the new one for special occasions. But thank you, Nancy. It's wonderful! Now, let's get breakfast and get down the road, shall we?" He placed the new hat back into the box and put his old one back on. As he was putting it back on he looked to make sure the map was still there. He could make it out. Everything was fine.

"Now, I could sure go for some bear and gravy for breakfast. How much meat did Mole leave us, Jake?" Thomas asked.

"He didn't leave us any. He said you got the hide and he got the meat. I guess it's plan ole' gravy and biscuits this morning," Jake said.

So the trio ate, packed up the wagon and headed down the dirt road. Again Thomas and Nancy were up front and Jake in the back of the wagon. The air was fresh from the rain and the wagon pushed onward toward Elkhorn.

It was about an hour before Nancy spoke up, "So, you really didn't like the hat did you? She asked.

"No, it's not that. It was a wonderful gift. It's just...," Nancy interrupted him. "You just don't like it. Just tell me. It's okay I'll understand."

Thomas pulled the wagon over to the side of the road and told Nancy to come with him. "Jake," Yelled Thomas.

"I need to walk on this leg some. Watch the horses will you? We'll be right back."

"Ya, sure thing. I need to go answer the call of nature anyway," Jake said.

Thomas took Nancy over to a meadow where they could still see the wagon. He leaned over to kiss her, but she turned and looked the other way.

"Listen, I guess I need to explain about the hat." Thomas thought should he tell her the whole story or just a part. After all, he had only known her for a few days. Thomas took off the old hat and turned it inside out.

"I know we said no secrets, but I do have one left," he said.

"What is it, Thomas?" Nancy asked in a concerned voice.

"I knew this man and I did a story on him. And before he died he told me about this map. A map that could take me on a treasure hunt. So after he died, I drew the map inside my old hat." Then Thomas showed the outline on the inside of his hat. "The treasure is supposed to be on Elkhorn Mountain. There might not be anything, but there might be everything. This key (he pulled it out of his shirt) opens a steel box that the map leads too. That is the real reason that I am on this trip. It's not to see any of my family. We know that is not true. It's to go on what I hope is not a wild goose chase."

Nancy turned back to Thomas. He held her close. "And besides if I hadn't come on this trip, we wouldn't have met. And I wouldn't be in love with you," Thomas ended.

Thomas kissed her and he noticed tears running down her face.

"What's wrong, Nancy?" he asked.

"I don't deserve this. You have been so kind to me. You're such a gentleman. And I am… well, I'm not real lady like. More like a tomboy. I guess now is a good time to tell you my last secret," She said.

She laid her head upon his chest. "Thomas, when I lived in Chester I had a husband and a son. I know that my husband died when the Crow came to town, because I buried him, but my son…Kyle was taken by the Crow. You see, I'm not as pure as you think. I'm a woman with alot of baggage. If you let me ride to Elkhorn with you, I'll keep your secret and not tell anyone."

Thomas looked down at her, "Nancy, I love you. Your past is behind you and the future lays ahead. I am truly sorry for the loss of your family. But let me ask you this, will you love me? We are standing under this mighty oak tree and in front of God and nature. So tell me,

Nancy, is there still love left in you heart for me? Is there room for me in your future?" Thomas asked.

"Yes, Thomas. Yes, there is love in my heart for you. There is alot of love for you, Thomas, but I'll have to warn you that at times I can be a little wild and crazy. Can you handle that?" She questioned.

"Oh I think I can handle that," He smiled back.

Thomas cupped her face in his hands and kissed her. Then he heard Jake yelling,

"You guys going to kiss all day or are we going to Elkhorn?"

"Shall we go treasure hunting, my lady?" Thomas asked.

"Lead on my gentleman. Lead on," Nancy said.

Jake had placed the bear hide on top of the wagon so the sun could cook the hide. As the wagon continued on, Thomas and Nancy became closer and the trip became longer.

They rode all day without another stop and came to the foothills of Elkhorn as the sun started to set. They set up camp and Jake and Thomas started supper while Nancy worked on the hide. Thomas looked and the pelt was coming along nicely. They sat around the fire and ate and talked.

"The deal was that I would go just to the mountain. So, I guess this is my last night with you two. I can't be your chaperone any longer," Jake laughed.

"Yes, that was the deal, but you are welcome to stay longer if you want," Thomas added.

"No, I traded most of the whiskey to Mole and I'm headed over to Spearfish in the morning. You're on your own, Mr. Bach, but I don't mind leaving you because your in good hands," Jake said.

"Well, good luck to you Jake. I wish you well. And by the way, nice shooting the other day and thank you," Thomas said.

They ate and turned in for the night. Thomas made up a bed beside the fire for him and Nancy. They let Jake sleep inside the wagon for the last night of his stay. Thomas and Nancy held each other as the night rolled in. The stars shone like bright beacons in the night. Thomas hoped the journey that lies ahead of them would soon be over.

"Do you ever wonder what it's all about?" Nancy asked.

"What are you talking about?" Thomas asked.

"Everything-the moon, the stars, the life we lead. What our kids will face?

What new things will happen in our life time? What's at the end of the universe?" Nancy said as she lay down and placed her head on Thomas's lap while she stared up at the stars.

"Well I'm not a genius, but I can safely say this," Thomas looked at Nancy, "Life is what you make it however long or short it is. You must make the best of it. Be the best person that you can be. One must not think about death, but live out their life caring about other people. Pass on your life lessons to the younger generations, so they can learn and grow. This nation is still growing there's no telling how far mankind will go." Thomas stated.

"Oh, I agree with you, Thomas. I see this nation… this world expanding and growing everyday. Cities and towns popping up everywhere. Before long there may be no room on earth. We may have to live on the moon!" Nancy said laughing.

Thomas leaned down and puts his chin on Nancy's shoulder.

"I wouldn't go that far. Humans are getting smarter. But the moon? I think that's just a little out of the reach of mankind. But I'll tell you what, right now in front of God and everyone. I'll sell you that moon," Thomas said.

"You're crazy! You can't own the moon!" Nancy exclaimed.

"Ah, but I do own the moon and I'll sell it to you. Look at it it's a full moon and it's just hanging in the sky. Waiting to be sold. What's my bid for this glorious moon? Stated Thomas.

"I'll give one kiss. One kiss that will hold us for a lifetime."

"Sold!" Thomas exclaimed.

And with that they kissed again as the moonlight fell into the night.

Thomas and Nancy lay quiet and held each other as the stars danced above their heads. While they watched the moon disappear over the horizon, Thomas looked at Nancy as she slept.

"Goodnight, Nancy. Your moon will soon be behind that mountain."

Chapter Four
"Company"

The night passed into morning. A heavy dew covered the ground and the sun shone through the trees. The sounds of the world were waking up. Thomas noticed a piece of paper stuck to the wagon seat. Slowly he took his arm from around Nancy and walked over to the note.

"You guys looked so peaceful, I didn't want to disturbed you. You're a nice man, Mr. Bach, and it has been quite a journey. I must be off to find my own way. You and Nancy will do fine. Until we meet again, good day to you Mr. Bach," signed Jake.

Thomas felt lost and a bit saddened. He also realized that for the first time he was solely responsible for someone else. He looked and saw Nancy laying on the bed. He went over to where she was laying and woke her up.

"Just how long can you sleep? I bet if I came back tonight you would still be laying here asleep," he said.

Nancy looked up. "I really do like my sleep, but I haven't slept like this in years," she said.

"Jake left sometime this morning. It's just you and me against the world. Think that you can handle it?" Thomas asked.

Nancy got up and started to get breakfast ready. Thomas could see that she was not herself this morning as she cooked over the fire. She seemed focused on something or somewhere else.

"What seems to be the matter, Nancy?" He asked.

"Oh, nothing. It's just that we are close to Chester. Some old feelings are coming up from down deep within me. I'll be fine. Don't worry; it will pass," she said.

"How far is Chester from here?" Thomas asked.

"Oh, it's about a half day's ride. Why?"

"Well, let's take a detour to Chester and get rid of some of your feelings. The map isn't going anywhere. It will be there when we get done," Thomas explained.

"Thomas, I can't have you do that. You have to follow through with what you came up here for," Nancy said.

"Let's eat and start to Chester. If you want to, I'll leave it up to you," Thomas said.

"It will take only a day to go and come back here. Thank you, Thomas! I need to heal some old wounds," Nancy said.

"That's fine. Let's get started with breakfast," he said.

Nancy went back to fixing breakfast and Thomas took off his boot to look at his leg. It was healing nicely but he knew he only had a few more days until he had to take out the stitches. Thomas applied some more salve to the cut and placed a fresh bandage on it. Nancy was calling that breakfast was done. They ate together, side by side. Thomas kept thinking in the back of his mind that the two of them were alone and he hoped that nothing would change that.

They ate and packed up the wagon. Nancy placed the bear hide back on top. She had just re-salted the hide. The sun was drying out the hide and slowly the smell was leaving. Nancy climbed up to the seat of the wagon and sat next to Thomas, holding him close. Thomas placed his spear up next to the front of the wagon, so anyone could see it. He hoped that if it had given Regan safe passage, it just might help them.

"Well which way, my lady?" Thomas asked.

"From here you just stay on this road and don't turn. This road goes right through Chester." Nancy said. So, Thomas slapped down the reins and off they went.

They rode about 4 hours and they didn't talk much. Then up ahead they saw the outline of a town. Nancy stood up and looked. "It's Chester. I can still see the church's steeple," she said.

The wagon meandered down the winding road toward Chester. As they entered the town, it was as Regan had described it. The houses were full of arrows and no one in sight.

"Go down this street. It's the last house on the right." Nancy said.

As the wagon pulled up to the front of the house, the horses got uneasy. The house was a modest, white with black shutters. It had a big yard with a white picket fence around it. The front door was busted in two and a few of the windows were broken. Nancy just sat there staring at the house. Thomas sat quietly for a moment.

"Would you like to go inside?" Thomas asked.

"Yes. Yes, I would," Nancy said in a strange low voice.

Nancy didn't take her eyes off the house as she jumped down from the seat. Thomas came up behind her and held her hand. They walked up to the porch and stopped. Nancy walked over to one of the broken windows and held onto one of the curtains that was blowing through it.

"These were given to me by my mother. She gave them to me on my wedding day. They rode all the way from Pennsylvania." Nancy turned toward Thomas with a half crocked smile. "My husband, Dale, built this house from lumber from our woods. It took him three years to get it done." Nancy looked down at the ground. "We slept in the barn until the house was done. The barn came with the property. Dale said that the livestock were our livelihood and that we should live there to watch over our herd. It seems so distant now. Like a wonderful dream."

Thomas held out his hand to Nancy and they walked into the house. The house looked really good for being vacant for a few years. They walked into the living room and Thomas noticed a few pictures that were still on the mantel above the fireplace. Nancy ran over and held the small one of her son.

"These were taken when he was five, about a year before the Crow came. Now he'd be almost nine. This is a picture of my husband and here is one of our wedding day. I really don't think you want to see all of these. I'm sorry," Nancy said.

"No. No. I'd like to see them. In fact, I think you should take them with you," Thomas looked into Nancy eyes, "So you can always remember and never forget."

The two walked through the house and Nancy gathered up some clothes and blankets and anything else she thought they might need. The Crow had taken only the food and any whiskey that they could find. Everything else was left just as it was. They loaded what they could into the wagon and Nancy said there was one more thing she wanted to get from upstairs. She ran up the steps and Thomas stood in the hallway. As Nancy came down the steps, Thomas heard a noise outside. It was one maybe two horses. Thomas approached the doorway with Nancy by his side. It was the Crow chief and a young brave. They were riding bareback and holding the reins of the horses. They just stared at Thomas and Nancy.

Thomas spoke first, taking off his hat, "May I help you?"

"We have been watching you for days. Where did you get that spear? And what are you doing on Crow land?" the chief commanded.

Thomas walked over to the spear and picked it up. "This was given to me by a good friend of both of ours. Mr. Regan Wright. I believe he returned your son to you after he was killed trying to steal horses. Regan said you were a great Chief and friend. He also said that if I carried this spear that no harm would come of me or my party. As to why we are here, this lady(Pointing to Nancy) owns this house. She is just here to get some of her belongings and then we are on our way," Thomas ended.

"Where is the man, Regan?" The Chief asked.

"They hanged him for something he didn't do. The white chief in Helena isn't as great as you are. He has no honor. This white chief speaks with wrong words. Lies and more lies. I am on a journey for Regan and it was a shame that they killed him. Regan was a good man."

The Chief raised his spear and from around the houses came at least 50 Indians, all on horseback. They looked worn and battered. They looked like they had been on the trail for a long time.

"I have many mouths to feed. My village grows large and one day we will take back this land. But today we must eat. The animals in this land have become few. The rains have come too late to plant. I must find a way to feed my people through the upcoming winter. It saddens me to know that Regan is dead. He was one of few white men that I trusted. He was an honorable man." Then the chief yelled and two braves came dragging a deer up to the house.

"Your wife will make supper for all. You will eat with us. Tonight we are friends, but never cross me or you will die," the chief commanded.

Thomas handed the spear back to the Chief. "I think that this belongs to you," He said.

"What do they call you?" The chief asked.

"My name is Thomas Bach and this is Nancy," Thomas spoke up.

"My name is Perits-Sinakpas, but you white men call me 'Medicine Crow," The chief explained.

The chief yelled again and the two riders with the deer rode to the back of the house to gut and cut it up. Thomas walked back to Nancy.

"It will be all right. Maybe we can learn something from them and maybe if we are nice they will tell us about your son," Thomas kissed Nancy on the cheek.

Thomas dug around in the back of his wagon. He hid the guns and found a few bottle of whiskey that Jake had missed. Thomas took his horses to the barn and penned them up for the night. He found some old grain that was still good and gave them fresh water. As he approached his wagon he noticed that Nancy had gotten out the cooking pots and was hauling them into the kitchen. Thomas helped her. She had already gotten a fire going in the stove. The Indians were outside getting the well pump to work. They finally got water to come out and kept pumping till the water was clear. They brought Nancy a few buckets of water.

"How does it feel to be cooking in your old kitchen again?" Thomas asked.

"I wish it was for just us, not the extra 50 uninvited guests." She placed her arms around Thomas and kissed him. "I was thinking that we may be here for longer than a half day. I'm so sorry that I had to get you in this mess."

"Hey, what mess? The Crow have been friendly and were having dinner with them tonight, aren't we Mrs. Bach?" Thomas grinned.

"Why, yes, we are, Mr. Bach," Nancy said as she kissed him again. "Now let me get busy. I have to make deer stew for around 60. This might take me awhile.

Thomas went back outside and the Indians had broken up a bunch of wooden chairs and placed tree branches in a big pile. Thomas thought that may be they were having a big bon fire later on that night. The chief crossed the road to meet Thomas.

"Let's go and talk some more, Thomas Bach," The chief said.

They walked into the old saloon and all the braves were in there. Thomas sat at a table that the chief had gestured to with his hand. Thomas listened to the chief ramble on about the white man taking all the land and that the land was owned by no one.

"Well, when I first saw you, you said that I was on Crow land. Doesn't that make you an owner of this land, like the white man?" Thomas asked.

"We are the land's people. We care for the land and it watches over our People," The chief said.

As the chief talked, the braves would yell and make noise when he stopped, like they were cheering him on. Thomas thought that he had better be careful not to take this too far.

"The white man came here and brought many others with him. They tore up the land by cutting down trees to make houses. They brought animals that eat to much grass, and they brought sickness to my people. I know in my heart of hearts that not all white men are evil. Regan had a good spirit. He walked among the white man, but he had the heart of a red man," The chief ended.

Thomas was thinking way a head of the chief and he got an idea, he hoped that it would work.

"How are you going to take care of your people this winter? How are you going to feed your village? Thomas asked.

"The Great Spirit will provide so my people will not go hungry. He will send a great man with many horses to help my people rise to fight again. Do not worry about us Thomas Bach, we will find a way," The chief concluded.

"Chief, let me ask you this. If you had enough money to buy food and anything that you might need, would you leave this land and go find greener pastures. Would you travel away from here, to free your people from an almost certain death?" Thomas asked.

"No man here has that kind of money. Do you have that kind of money Thomas Bach?" The chief asked.

"I think we need to talk alone chief," he said.

The chief yelled for everyone to leave except for two braves. They came over and sat beside the chief at the table.

"These are my sons. You can say whatever you need to say; they will not tell," the chief said.

"The journey that I am on is really a treasure hunt. Regan told me where it is and I am on the trail to find it. If you help me, I will give you half the money for the purchase of this town and the land around it. You are to take the money leave town and let this town start to grow again. You will have enough money to buy lots of land for your families-for you village," Thomas ended.

The chief sat there very quiet. He leaned over to one of his sons and said something. They talked back and forth for a moment. Then the chief looked at Thomas.

"Why would you do this? Why would you give the Crow half your money?" the chief asked.

"I would do this for a couple of reasons. First, I would do it for the friendship of Regan that we both share. Second, it would benefit both of us. I also would want a few things in exchange," Thomas stated.

"What would you need, Thomas Bach?" He asked.

"I would like a few braves to escort me to Elkhorn to get the money. And then I would want you to give back Nancy's young boy. When you raided this town you took him with you. Do you still have him?" Thomas asked.

"We have many boys from this town; they learn the ways of the Crow. Isn't this boy also yours?" the chief questions.

"Nancy and I are not married. We met on the trail and fell in love. I would like to marry her, but I can't find a preacher way out here. The boy you have is her son. The boys father was killed in the raid," Thomas said.

The chief conferred with his sons and one was very angry. He slammed down his fist and yelled some things that Thomas didn't understand. The chief pointed to the door and the brave left. The chief stared at Thomas.

"We will give back the boy when you return with the money. We have a deal Thomas Bach? Don't try to back out of it. I will give you 3 braves to follow you to the money. When you return, we will open the box together, count together and share together. Tonight if you want, we will wed you and Nancy in our native ceremony. You will be married in this life time and in the next. Let me know by morning," the chief ended.

Thomas stood up and held out his hand. The chief shook his hand and Thomas said, "It's a deal. But, there is one problem Chief. The first box must be opened so that I may use the map to find the real box," Thomas added.

"That is fine. The second box will not be opened until it is returned to town." The chief then left the saloon

Thomas departed also and walked across to Nancy's house and into the kitchen. Nancy was busy cooking in 4 large pots and checking the oven.

"Nancy, can I ask you a question?" he said.

"I guess so, but I'm really busy." she said.

"Do you love me? I mean really love me," He Questioned.

Nancy stopped in her tracks and looked at Thomas. "Oh, I love you. These last couple of days it has grown into have a deep love. Why do you ask?" she questioned.

"Because I would like to marry you. I would like to marry you tonight under these stars," Thomas blurted out.

Nancy just stood there with her eyes wide open. Her mouth dropped open and she just stared at Thomas. "Are you serious? Who would be the preacher? Do I have a dress to wear? This is all so sudden. Why, yes, I'll marry you... yes, yes, a thousand times yes!" She jumped into Thomas's arms and they kissed.

"The Chief will marry us tonight if I tell him. Shall I tell him yes? Thomas asked.

"Yes Thomas and I want to be married in front of this house." she said.

"There's more to tell you, but that can wait until tonight," Thomas kissed her again and went out the back door to tell the chief.

Nancy felt like she was drunk on whiskey. Her heart was beating fast and her head was spinning. She loved Thomas and she wanted to stay in her house and start over. She hadn't planned it like this, but she had wished it would just happen someday. She had wished that one day she would return to Chester and get a second chance.

Thomas walked down the town streets looking for the chief. He saw him standing next to the saloon talking to some young braves. The chief looked over at Thomas.

"She said yes," Thomas yelled, "tonight would be great!"

Chief Medicine Crow clapped his hand three times and two braves followed him across the street to Thomas. Chief Medicine Crow signaled with his left hand and one of the braves climbed onto a horse and rode off.

"He has gone to get the mothers of our village, to help prepare your woman for marriage," Medicine Crow said.

Just then Thomas heard Nancy, "Come and get it! Everyone can come in the kitchen door and can leave though the front door. The Chief yelled and his braves all ran to the back door. "I will eat after my brothers, but before the women," the chief explained.

As they were walking around the back of the house, Thomas saw the brave on horse back followed by the women of the village. Meanwhile, Nancy was dipping out stew and bread to the line of Indians. She had gotten together plates and silverware from the other houses. She was hoping that it would be enough. The Chief entered the line dividing the men from the women. He turned and talked to the line of squaws as they nodded their heads. When the chief got to the kitchen he held out his plate. Nancy dipped one scoop onto the chief's tray and layed a slice of bread next to it. She started to dip another and the chief spoke up.

"I get the same as everyone else. No more, no less," he said.

When the line was done, there was just enough left for Thomas and Nancy. They ate at the kitchen table. When they were done, the chief entered the kitchen with one brave and two older women.

"We will have the wedding when the moon reaches the highest point in the sky," he said.

Thomas looked at Nancy one last time before the brave took him by the arm and walked him out of the kitchen. He was led down the main street, across an open meadow until they reached a rough looking Indian village. The village was in major disrepair. There were big holes in the teepees and some had fallen down. Thomas thought to himself that the town looked just like the Crow-rundown and tired. He also noticed that they didn't have much meat drying in the sun. Perhaps it was a good thing that Thomas had come on this adventure. The braves led Thomas into a large wigwam and sat him down on a deerskin rug. Two older squaws entered the room carrying a set of buckskins and a bowl of water.

"Take off your clothes," ordered the one brave.

Thomas disrobed and sat back down on the rug. Then the two squaws washed Thomas and rubbed him down some oils. The one Indian brave said something to everyone and Thomas was left alone. He took the clothes that they had laid before him and put them on. They were a little loose and the pant legs didn't reach all the way down. Then one of the older squaws reentered again carrying a cloth and a wooden jar. She took his leg and looked at the large bear claw mark. She took the jar and applied a salve to the cut. Thomas's face contorted in pain. As the sting of the salve wore off, the squaw laughed at him and took a cloth and wrapped his leg.

Thomas sat there waiting and then the chief came into the room. He carried a few items in a leather pouch. He opened the pouch and took out a small metal pot and some dried leaves. He then took out a smaller leather pouch that looked like it was smoking. The pouch contained a few small hot coals from a fire. He placed the coals into the pot and then put in the leaves. He blew into the pot and a fire started. He then placed some moss into the pot and smoke started to fill the room.

"Thomas Bach, lean into the smoke and breath. I will place the powder of our Fathers into the flame. When you breath you will close your eyes and see your life path. You may also see your future," the chief said.

Thomas leaned over the pot and the chief placed the powder into the flames. The blue flames changed to red and then to yellow. Thomas breathed deeply once, twice and then he fell back onto the rug. His mind was flashing brilliant colors. He kept his eyes closed and he could hear the chief singing in the background. Thomas felt a strange pressure on his brain as the colors turned into faces that flashed across his mind and then disappeared. He saw Nancy, Jake and his foster parents. The faces slowly disappeared and then he saw black. In the distance he could make out two people fighting. As the images got closer, he could see that it was an Indian that was stabbing a white man. The images flew forward of Thomas. Thomas looked down the Indian was gone. The white man who lay dying was Jake. The Indian had killed his friend Jake. Jake was trying to say something to Thomas.

"I'm sorry. I'm sorry for killing… I'm sorry for…" then Jake died.

Thomas sat up at looked around, but nobody was there. Sweat ran down his face and he struggled to get up. He noticed that the teepee door was open, so he crawled out. When he stood up the, chief was looking at him face to face.

"You may have questions. Your path will answer them. Time is your friend and always speak the truth," the chief said.

The chief bolstered Thomas as they walked back to town. Thomas became more awake and more his old self. They walked down the main street to the front of Nancy's house. Then an older Indian appeared in the doorway.

"This is my father, Timber Wolf. I have told him of our trade and he thinks that it is a good one. He says that I must make this trade for the good of my people. He will be the one joining your life paths tonight," the chief said.

Timber Wolf carried two strips of leather, one black and one red. He layed them over Thomas's shoulders. He then turned and started to talk in Crow.

"I will repeat what Timber Wolf says in the white man's tongue," said the chief.

Thomas looked up and saw Nancy walking through the door. His jaw fell open and his eyes got big. She was, beautiful!

"My God! You are absolutely stunning," he said out loud.

Nancy was dressed in a formal gown with white lace. It was also trimmed with feathers.

"I guess we owe someone for this dress. I took it from one of the shops in town," Nancy said.

"That's fine. It's worth every penny," Thomas stammered.

Timber Wolf motioned for Thomas and Nancy to stand side by side. As he spoke the Chief interpreted.

"The wind, Mother Earth, Sun, Moon and Stars. We are all a part of this. The life we take travels down many paths. Some good, some not."

Timber wolf grabbed the right hand of Thomas and placed it on top of Nancy's left hand. He then took both leather straps from Thomas.

"These straps represent the bond between two souls. The black one is for the unknown travels that you will take on your life path."

Timber Wolf took the black strap and tied it around both Thomas' and Nancy's hands.

"This red strap is the blood bond between two souls. The blood of your two families joining as one. The blood of your children and their children."

He took the red strap and tied it on top of the black one. Timber Wolf signaled with his hands and the two older squaws appeared behind Thomas and Nancy carrying the bear hide.

"I had my Village finish this hide for you as a gift," The chief said.

"Thank you," Thomas said.

The squaws placed it over both Thomas and Nancy, resting the top on their heads.

"This hide shall bond you together. With it you shall enter the same life path but to do so you must have new names. Thomas Bach, your new name is 'Thomas Claw.' The bear has marked you and his spirit fills your body. He will rise again when needed. Nancy, your new name is 'Morning Fawn,' because of your bright eyes and your willingness to follow a new path. These names carry them to your graves and now you may start on your path."

Thomas turned to Nancy and kissed her. He could hear the yips and screams of the Indians. He turned around and saw that the house had been laced with a path of flower petals and feathers that traced the main room and went up the stairs. The two walked the path up the stairs and went into the master bedroom. Thomas opened the door.

"Just give me a few minutes and you can come in," Nancy said.

Thomas walked over to the window and saw that the Crow had stated a fire. They were in for a big celebration tonight. Thomas had given the Chief the last of the whiskey bottles from his wagon and they were dancing around the fire and having a good time.

"Thomas Claw," Nancy called through the door.

"Coming," Thomas said.

Thomas approached the door and with one hand pushed it open. The room was filled with candles; they flickered dancing across the room. Nancy was laying on the bed and the only thing she was wearing was the bear skin.

"Well, Thomas Claw are you just going to stand there and stare or are you going to close the door and make love to me?" She questioned.

In a low voice, Thomas replied, "Yes, ma'am. I always listen to ladies that wear bear hide nightgowns." And Thomas did just that.

Chapter Five
The Metal Box

Nancy awoke embraced in Thomas's arms. The sun was just coming in through the bedroom window. She watched Thomas sleep and her mind wondered. She looked around the room and she saw everything from her old life. Photographs, clothes and memories lined the room. She slowly climbed out of bed and put her nightgown on. She took a basket from the closet and started to fill it with the mementos of her past. Piece by piece she laid them into the basket and placed it back into the closet. The only keepsake that she left was a photo of her son. She crossed over to Thomas's side of the bed and knelt beside him on the floor.

"Are you going to sleep all day?' She asked.

Thomas opened his eyes and looked at her. He placed his hand on her cheek and kissed her lightly on the forehead.

"Are you sorry, now that it is morning?" He asked

"I'll never be sorry. I just wish that last night and today could last forever. I'll be sorry only when you to leave," She added.

Thomas sat up in bed. "We really need to talk," he said. Thomas explained the deal that he had made with the chief. He also told her that the Chief had said that her son was alive and well. All Thomas has to do is get to the treasure and make it back again.

"It sounds good, but what if I lose you. What happens to me Thomas? What will I do? And I don't think that I can start over again," she said laying down beside of Thomas.

"It will all work out, Nancy. You will see. And if something should happen to me, you could always move in with your son. This is something I need to do for us as well as the Crow," Thomas ended.

They laid together and talked until they heard noises coming from downstairs. Thomas got up and dressed and climbed down the staircase. Standing by the front door was the chief and three of his braves.

"I will give you these three braves to help you on your journey. Morning Fawn shall stay here until you return or the braves return."

Thomas looked at his braves. They were strong and young. "We will need to dress them like a white man. If they go out looking like this and we should run into someone, it could be really bad for them," He added.

The chief agreed and sent them off to one of the old stores to find and dress like the white man. Nancy came down the stairs and watched as Thomas and the chief hooked up the horse team and loaded the wagon with supplies. Thomas found his gun and strapped his colt to his side. He crossed back to the house and saw Nancy standing on the porch.

"So, I guess this is it. You are going and there is no stopping you," Nancy said.

"Yes, we are going in a few minutes. The sooner we leave, the sooner I will get back and we will start our lives together," Thomas said as he kissed her.

The braves came back dressed in jeans and wool shirts. The two climbed into the back and one rode on a horse, beside the wagon.

Thomas sat down and grabbed the reins and looked back at Nancy. He slapped down the on the horses and off the wagon went. Tears ran down Nancy's face as the wagon rode off. The chief walked up behind her and placed his hands on her shoulders.

"He is a good man. Good men never die; you shouldn't worry. Besides my braves were told, that they would die before Thomas Claw," The chief said.

Thomas held the reins tightly as the wagon rolled down the dusty road. His mind wandered back to Nancy. He thought to himself about how they had just got together and now they were apart. This was hard for Thomas. He had never felt like this before; he had never really loved anyone like Nancy before. He wanted to turn around and yell back to her, but he kept a straight line between him and Elkhorn.

All he had to do was get to Elkhorn and then back to Chester and then spend the rest of his life loving Nancy. Thomas took off his hat and looked up and prayed, "Lord, let me know if I should turn back now and forget this whole thing. I pray that the money is still there and everything falls into place. I'll leave it in Your hands."

And with that he placed his hat back on his head looking briefly at the map as he did.

Thomas looked into the back of the wagon after it had gotten out of site of Chester. The braves were sleeping side by side. To his left, to one brave rode his horse bareback, to keep a close eye on Thomas and the wagon.

They rode on for about 5 hours. Thomas stopped the wagon near where he had camped before.

Thomas looked at the brave riding beside him and said. "This is where I ran into the bear the last time I camped here." With that Thomas made a growl and lifted up his pant leg to exposed his healing wound.

"We will get water for the horses and rest awhile. Wake your buddies up and let's get this done."

The brave just looked at Thomas. Thomas thought, "This maybe a little harder than I thought."

Thomas pounded on the side on the wagon as he climbed down from the seat. One by one the braves stumbled out of the back and as they stood up, the brave on the horse gave them orders and they unhooked the horses and walked them down the path to the river. This area looked familiar to Thomas. He walked over to where Moe's wagon had been parked and he noticed the tracks were gone but in their place were many sets of horse prints. He knelt down and looked closely at the tracks. They were deep and imbedded into the ground, like the horses rode hard and fast down the road. As Thomas looked over the tracks, he heard the braves making a loud noise. Thomas stood up and looked over. The braves were waving at him to come over. They were standing in waist high brush and pointing at something on the ground. As Thomas walked over to the braves, the closer he got the worse the smell was. Thomas grabbed the kerchief form his back pocket and placed it over his face.

"Is it a dead deer?" Thomas asked.

Thomas looked at the feet of the braves and their laying on the ground was a dead white man. Thomas was stunned. Something was very wrong here. The clothes looked familiar.

"Oh my God!" Thomas yelled as he knelt down and turned over the body. It was Mole. He had been shot in the back and left for dead.

"Do you know this white man?" The main brave asked.

"You speak English! You speak English and this is the first thing you say to me? Yes. Yes, I know this man. He wouldn't hurt anyone. And someone shot him in the back." Thomas exclaims, "We have to bury him. We have to give him a decent burial. We are not going to leave him here for the animals to eat."

"Thomas Claw, I am sorry for not talking sooner, but I was told not to until I had to. I am Cheete, but you can call me Wolf. And these are my brother, Iaxuhke, Red fox and my youngest brother Iishbiia or Puma. We will dig a grave for your friend, just show us where."

It took Thomas a few minutes to get his head straight. He walked over to where a clearing was and looked out over the mountain. "Here, dig here and we will face him to the hills that he loved so much."

The braves took the tools out of the wagon and started to dig the grave. Thomas went back over to Mole and looked over his body. He did notice a few things. Mole had his gold pocket watch and his wallet still had his money in it. Everything seemed in order. Thomas placed the pocket watch in his pocket and took the money from the wallet.

He crossed back over to the braves who were just finishing up with the grave. Thomas handed them the cash and Wolf just looked at him. "Don't worry, Wolf. He'll never miss it. Besides, it's payment for a job well done."

The men carried Mole over and place him in the soil. Thomas took off his hat and spoke, "I don't know much about this man, but what I do know was that he was fair. A good man of these mountains. Mole, may you rest in peace knowing that I will find the people that put you here. I will find them and they will be brought to justice. May God find a special place for you," and with that the men settled the earth upon Mole. Thomas made a cross of branches latched together with Mole suspenders and he drove it into the ground, as a makeshift head stone.

Thomas walked back to the wagon and he looked into the west sky. "Lets set up camp here for the night, but be on guard. There is no telling who is watching us or what they want," Thomas said.

He took down his pack and started to sort things out while the braves gathered wood for a fire. Thomas felt uneasy again as he walked to the edge of the fork in the road. One fork led to Chester and one led to Helena, The one in the middle, that was rough and worn. The road that had been washed out several times by water, was the base of Elkhorn mountain. Thomas just looked at the road, he then took off his hat and looked down. The map was still intact and looking at it made it seem all to real. His journey had taken him to new places and to meet people that he wouldn't have met on his own. And Nancy… he couldn't keep his mind off of her. "Thomas, you are a married man. You need to do this for the future of your family and for the families of the Indians. In a matter of weeks, my life has changed... but change is good," he talked to himself.

"Claw!" yelled Wolf.

Thomas turned and Wolf was holding up two very large rabbits. He walked over to the braves.

"Well, it looks like we eat good tonight. Doesn't it fellas." Thomas said laughing.

Thomas built up the fire and the braves brought over the rabbits and started to cook them. They sat around the fire as the sun set and the night grew colder. They ate and Thomas watched the fire as it crackled and spit. The braves were telling stories of days past and Thomas watched as they mimicked a hunt. Thomas was still felt uneasy about everything. He was worrying about Nancy and thought of poor Mole.

He laid his bed out and layed his head on a pillow that he had taken from the house. Thomas stared at the stars. "They seem so close tonight." he thought and then he saw the moon. "Ah, Nancy's moon," he smiled and with that he closed his eyes and left the braves to their stories. Thomas fell asleep to the dances in the night, both in the sky and by the campfire.

He slept until the early morning. The sun hadn't risen yet and Thomas noticed that his fire had gone out in the night. He stood up and walked to bushes to answer the call of nature. As he was finishing up, he could see something on the other side of the mountain. Thomas walked through the thicket and knelt close to the ground. It was about 2 miles away but Thomas could make out a campfire. As he went to stand up, a hand pushed him back down.

It was Wolf. "Claw, we must move on. It is not safe here."

"Wolf, how long have they been here?" Thomas asked.

"We saw them last night. I went up to their wagon. 6 men all drinking whiskey, firing guns, all sleeping by dusk. All carrying guns and one wears the pointed sun on his chest," Wolf stated.

"A pointed sun... you mean a star? Thomas whispered.

"Yes."

"Yeah you are right let's get out of here!"

And with that Thomas and the braves gathered up everything, hooked up the team of horses and under the cover of the early morning darkness started their climb up Elkhorn.

About and hour into the climb, the sun started to peek the ridges and shine on the mountain. The sun was to their backs, but all Thomas was thinking was about the men that were behind them. Were they just there for some other reason or were they following them? The wagon came upon a clearing and a grassy area with a small lake. Thomas yelled at Wolf to unhitch the team and let them eat and drink. "There's no telling if there is food or water up ahead."

"Claw, I will send Red Fox back to see if the men are following us or not," Wolf said.

"That would be a good idea," Thomas said. "I'll get us something to eat. We also need to eat and drink. We will also need fresh water in the barrel."

Wolf yipped to his brothers and they started to unload the water barrel and dump out the old water for fresh. Thomas crossed to the back of the wagon and got out the evening meal. In a large burlap bag was enough biscuits to feed an army. He then took out the dried meat strips and grabbed the cooking pots. As he turned he could see that the braves already had a fire going. Thomas sat the tripod up and hooked the kettle to the chain. He poured in the water and then threw in the meat strips. Flour, salt and wild herbs followed. Thomas watched as the water came to a boil. As he stirred the mix, Wolf came riding up.

"The men have camped for the night. They have tied up their horses and pitched tents along the road," Wolf said.

"Why would they set up camp this early? It can't be more than noon. Unless they are planning to ride at night. Where is Red Fox?" Thomas asked.

"He has not returned. We will wait until after we eat, then we must move on. Red Fox can catch up to us later. Do not worry about Red

Fox. He can take care of himself. But I do believe that the 6 white men are following us. We will have to stay at least a ½ day ahead of them," Wolf Explained.

"Oh, I agree with you one hundred percent. Come, lets eat and call your brother,"' Thomas said.

No one said a word as they ate. Thomas glanced down at the fire and his thought were once again on Nancy. He worried about her and hoped that this would be over soon, but something deep inside Thomas echoed the warning's of things to come. He stood up and took off his belt and hat.

"Wolf come with me," Thomas stated. "In the bottom of my hat is the map to where the 1st box is buried. The count measurements are laid out in my belt. See, this is how it works." Thomas showed Wolf the hat and belt. "If anything should happen to me, remember this is where the information to the money is. And you are to give Nancy my half. Do we have an understanding?"

Wolf nodded his head and shook Thomas's hand.

"Now we have to find this side road that is ¾ of the way up this mountain. This road goes to the right and comes to an open field. At the end of this field is a large rock shaped like a arrowhead. Then we apply the distances that appear on the belt. We must follow the belt in order from the buckle down to the end. L meaning left and R meaning right, But it is imperative that we find this Arrowhead shaped rock. It is very large according to Reagan." Thomas explained.

Wolf got a long look on his face and turned away from Thomas. He picked up a blade of grass and looked down, then looks at the sky.

"What is wrong, Wolf? Was it something that I said?" Thomas asked.

"No, Thomas Claw, but what you are asking is a fool's journey," Wolf states.

"What are you talking about. Everything was fine just a few minutes ago. What did I say?" Thomas asked.

"It is not exactly everything you said. It was very smart of you to write down the map and directions on your hat and belt. No one would look for them there."

"Then what for God's sake is the matter? We both have alot at stake here!" Thomas was yelling.

Wolf turned and faces Thomas. "I Know where this arrowhead rock is that you seek. It is the entrance to the Siksika. And no one shall enter there without being Siksika or they will never see the next morning sunrise," Wolf explains.

"The Siksika. I have never heard of them. They can't be that large of a group of Indians. Can't you just talk to them and explain to them what we are doing?" Thomas asks.

"The white men call the Siksika the Blackfoot. There numbers are large and the Crow's people really don't get along with them. They don't get along with anyone, and one does not just walk up and talk to them, Thomas Claw" Wolf yelled back.

"Blackfoot. My God Wolf what will we do? According to the map the 1st box is 102 chains SE to the water falls." Thomas knelt on the ground and grabbed a small stick and started to figure out the distance.

"Let's see one chain is 66 feet and 80 chains are equal to one mile so we are looking at about 1 ¼ miles from the rock to the box. That's not too bad. We should be able to find it and get out before we are noticed. What do you think Wolf? Can we do this or should we return to Chester and get others?

"What you seek Thomas Claw is a very dangerous path. And no, we can not return to Chester. Our people need us to finish this journey. We will pack up and start the climb again. When we get to the road we will see what the Great Father tells us," Wolf says.

They both walked to the wagon and still there was no sign of Red Fox. Wolf talks to his brother as they pack up and douses the fire by placing mud then dry dirt over the old camp fire. The horses were hooked up and Thomas climbed aboard and started up the mountain. Wolf hung back behind the wagon and talked to his brother. Wolf stayed behind the wagon as it made its way up the dirt road.

“Blackfoot... Regan. (Thomas looked to the sky) I take it that you didn’t know anything about this or did you leave that little tid-bit out of your story. I hope you keep an eye on me Regan. I may need you later on,” Thomas laughs out loud.

The late July sun beat down on the wagon as it crept along the road. As the wagon came to a right turn in the road, Thomas stopped to wagon and called Wolf.

“Is this the one Wolf?” Thomas asked

“This road is one way to the rock, but it is more of a hunting trail. The wagon will get stuck a little way down and you cannot turn around. You must go through. The mountain waters flood and keep the road wet and in deep mud,” Wolf explains.

“Really I have a plan. Does your brother know where the rock is? Can they find it? Thomas asked.

“Yes, we have hunted on the boarder for many years. Why?” Wolf asked.

“Everyone come here. Gather round. This is what we are going to do,” Thomas explains his plan.

“Wolf, you will follow me further up the mountain. Puma will take the two spare wagon wheels and start down the path making tracks in the dirt and mud. Hopefully the other wagon will follow and get stuck. We will meet your brothers at the rock before sunset. How does that sound? Thomas said smiling.

Wolf and his brother just grinned. So Puma took the wheels and started down the wrong path. Wolf stayed behind Thomas’s wagon and with a tree branch wiped away Thomas’s tracks. The two worked their way up the mountain until Thomas saw another right in the road that was twice a wide as the other one.

“How far to the rock, Wolf ?

“It is about one mile. This road will bare to the right and there is a steep downhill for about ¼ mile. I hope the brakes work good on that wagon,” Wolf said laughing.

“Good brakes and good horses, we should be okay, but thanks for asking,” Thomas said laughing back.

They came to the downhill part as the sun was clearing the hilltop. The wagon crept along and to the right with out a hitch. The big horses held back the wagon and Thomas only rode the brake a little. As dusk settled they came to the rock. Laying beside the rock was the wagon wheels and Puma.

"Are we to set up camp here for the night, Thomas Claw? Wolf asked.

"I really don't see how we can measure out the distance in the dark. I don't want to use a torch because everyone will see it. So, I guess we set up camp behind the rock next to the woods and no fire. As soon as the sun starts to rise in the morning we start then just get it done and over with. Then off to the real box. So does it sound like a plan? Thomas queried.

The braves agreed and Thomas climbed into the wagon and laid down to sleep. He wasn't asleep for very long when he heard a weird noise outside the wagon. He peeked out of a flap in the wagon holding his colt revolver. He saw Wolf and his brother sitting in a circle wiping something on their faces and down their arms. They were singing in a low voice and rocking back and forth. Thomas closed the flap and laid back down. The next thing he knew it was early morning and Wolf was whispering out his name.

"Yes, I'm coming. Just give me a minute."

As Thomas climbed out of the wagon, the braves laughed and pointed to his face.

"What is the matter, why are they pointing at me Wolf? Thomas asked.

"My brother painted your face to help protect you from the evil that lives on this mountain. Take this rabbit pelt and wipe your face. Bury the pelt in a spot that you like. This will give you safe travel," Wolf explained.

Thomas wiped his face and placed the pelt into his pocket. He looked up and the sun was coming through the trees. Daylight shown onto the wagon and Thomas stood up and stretched.

"Well, it's time to mark off this 102 chains, Wolf."

As the sun hit the arrowhead rock Thomas looked at it's grandeur and noticed the cut marks in the rocks.

"Did they carve the rock, Wolf?" Thomas questioned.

"They say that it took 20 braves 1 year to shape this rock. This rock points to their burial grounds," Wolf explained.

Thomas placed his back to the rock, looked into his bag and took out his compass. He placed the compass on SE, took off his belt and hat and started to walk off the 102 chains. He remembered a few small words that was on the map before he burnt it up. *Burford White* were the words and *8:30*. Thomas didn't know what they meant but the time was it AM or PM?

So off they went, Thomas leading the way. He kept looking down at his compass and then the hat and belt. The braves smiled as they walked though the woods. This went on for hours. It just didn't fall into place as Thomas had thought. This wasn't going to be easy. The men crossed into a clearing and then Thomas heard the river. They stopped by the river and then followed it downstream to the falls. Thomas turned and faced the area where they had come. He could see the arrowhead rock. It stood out in a clearing on a hill, rising above the trees in the lower land. Thomas looked at his watch 8:10 am. He looked at the rock and then to his compass. Thomas sat down on a log and looked at the braves.

"Well, we might have to pack a lunch. This may take us days to figure out," Thomas said.

"But Claw, we don't have days. We have only hours and we need to get this done and move on," Wolf said.

Thomas looked into his bag. He kept looking and digging. He sat up and looked at the braves.

"This is all that I have. The measurement to the box and this key." He held up his necklace. "I just don't know. I just don't know Wolf. You and your brother need to go and move the wagon and horses closer. We will need to hide the wagon and tie up the horses," Thomas said.

"Claw, we will do as you say. But you must try again to solve this. You must fine this box of ours." And with that Wolf and his brothers left.

Thomas took out his pelt and went to the edge of the river and placed it under a large rock. He sat down on the rock and looked over the fallwater. It was then that he saw a beautiful swatch of white flowers. They seemed to be planted all in one patch. Thomas looked for other plants like these. He could not find any.

"Nancy would like these flowers," He thought. "They are really white and…" Suddenly Thomas took out his compass and stood behind the patch of flowers and pointed it to the arrowhead. The needle pointed SE. "*Burford White,*" Thomas thought to himself. Thomas fell to his knees and started to dig up the flowers. He dug with his bare hands. The ground seemed loose and fresh. He dug deeper until he had reached a flat river rock. Thomas went to his bag and took out a small handpick, and started to hammer it into the rock. He dug around the rock and edged the rock on it's side. Sweat was running down his face as he lifted the rock out of the hole. Thomas looked into the hole and saw a small box covered in dirt and mud. With one large heave, he lifted the box out of the hole and looking into the sky.

"Regan, you ole' friend. Why didn't you tell me that Burford White was a flower? You kinda left that out," Thomas smiled and laughed out loud. It was then Thomas's bad feeling had came over him.

"Click!"

Thomas turned and saw a colt bearing down on him. His eyes moved up the arm and what he saw set him falling back to the ground.

"Jake? Jake, what are you doing."

"The great Thomas Bach. Not looking too great now are we. Where are you friends, Mr. Bach? It looks like just me and you and I'm carrying the high ace. Now get away from that box so I can open it and get what's mine."

"And mine"

Thomas turned and looked to his right and there was the Sheriff of Helena and the rest of the men.

"Well, well Mr. Bach. We have been following you for weeks. Oh, let me introduce myself. Robert McKenzie, Sheriff McKenzie. And I do believe that you have my box of money."

"It doesn't have any cash in it. It is just some more things of Regan's," Thomas said.

The men all laughed.

"How dumb do you think I am Bach? You haven't figured it out yet have you? You were set up. You walked right into my trap. You even helped me. Ole Jake here was going to follow you out of town and meet you on the trail. Instead you hired him for god sake. He works for me. Man, are you dumb, for a smart man," McKenzie explains.

"What about Mole?" Thomas asked.

"Mole got just what he deserved. He figured out what was going on and was going to tell you, But Jake here shut him up. Didn't ya, Jake?" McKenzie laughed.

"Yes, sir. I just picked his brain a little," All the men laughed.

"Now open up the damn box Bach!" McKenzie yelled.

As Thomas sat up he noticed the braves standing behind the Sheriff in the bushes. Thomas picked up the box and turned it on its side. He dug into his bag. The men pulled up their guns.

"Nothing fancy Bach. Slow and easy," McKenzie drawled.

Thomas pulled out a brush and cleaned off the keyhole. He took the necklace off and placed the key into the lock. As he turned the key the men leaned into Thomas to see what was inside. The lock clicked and the top opened up. Everything was in there that Regan said would be: Compass, eyescope, bag of gold containing $700.00 and a map. Thomas wadded up the map in his hand and with his other hand turned the box around.

"Here is your blood money, Sheriff. All $700.00 of it."

Thomas threw it at the Sheriff's feet.

"What the hell." Yelled McKenzie as he drew his weapon on Thomas.

It was then that Thomas heard the sound of swift air moving. One of McKenzie's men hit the dirt with an arrow sticking out of him.

"Indians!" Yelled McKenzie.

McKenzie turned and started firing his gun into the woods.

Thomas crawled to his gun as Red Fox jumped into the middle of the men and started fighting. Wolf and Puma had killed 3 of the others and out of the corner of Thomas's eye he saw an Indian grab a hold of Jake and roll him into the brush. Thomas ran to catch up as Red Fox stabbed Jake in the chest. Jake turned and looked into Thomas's eyes.

"I'm sorry for killing Mole, Thomas," Jake whispers as Red Fox sliced his throat.

Thomas looked around him. It was all over. All the white men were dead. Sheriff McKenzie lay in a pool of blood with an arrow in his chest. It was then Thomas realized just how savage the braves could be. That was lucky for him.

"Claw, are you all right?" Wolf questioned.

"Yes, I'm fine. Red Fox, you found us," Thomas said.

"Do you have the map?" Wolf asked.

Thomas looked into his hand at the paper.

"Yes, I think. Yes," Thomas stated.

It was then that Thomas unrolled the paper. It was a map that started at the arrowhead rock. It had measurements and a saying written on it.

"Walk through the Heart of the Arrow N/W and see the graves of friends. MAF."

Thomas read it out loud and Wolf just looked at him.

"Why can't you white men ever just say where something is going to be. Instead you must make us wander around in dangerous lands. We must go now. These, white men fired their guns and the Blackfoot will be here soon. Thomas, help me and my brothers push the bodies into the river and over the falls," Wolf said.

They pushed the dead men into the river and collected the box and bag. Then they headed up to the wagon, which was downhill from the arrowhead rock. Red Fox came walking up to the wagon leading 4 horses. He talked to his brothers and they laughed.

"What is so funny, Wolf?" Thomas asked.

"The other horses took off and their wagon is stuck in the mud on the road." Wolf said.

Thomas grinned and then turned his attention back to the map. *"Walk through the Heart of the Arrow N/W and see the graves of friends. MAF."*

Thomas looked at Wolf.

"Wolf didn't you say the rock had a heart," Thomas asked.

"Thomas, do you know what you are asking? That will take us deep into Blackfoot land. How many chains, Claw? How many chains?" Wolf asked.

"Well according to this…206. It's around 2 1/5 miles, give or take." Thomas said.

"Sounds like more give than take, Claw. I will talk to my brothers. We will need to ready ourselves for this trek across Siksika land. Maybe you need to ready yourself also, Thomas claw," Wolf said.

Thomas gathered up all the supplies and placed them into the wagon. He reined up the horses, tying them off to an oak tree. Thomas stood there leaning against this tree. He thought back to Jake and how he had seen this before in his dream. He knew he must push on into dangerous territories, which held the unknown. The last thing he put into his wagon was the small steel box. He took out the gold and placed half the gold coins into a small bag. The rest he put back into the box.

Wolf and his brothers came riding their new horses down the path. Their faces were painted in blue and white. They circled the wagon.

"Wolf. Here is your share of the money so far. It is half," Thomas then threw the bag so Wolf could catch it. Wolf placed it into his saddle bag.

"You are a good man, Thomas Claw. We will try to protect you as we move on through the Siksika territories. I hope you will also, how do you white men say, watch my back?" Wolf said.

Nothing else needed to be said as they started down the road beyond the arrowhead rock.

Chapter Six
Keeping House

Nancy watched as Thomas and the wagon drifted off into the distance. The wagon rolled down the dirt road leaving a dust trail. Nancy looked down at the floor of the front porch. It was then she realized that once again she was alone. She had no one by her side, no one to talk too, other than the Indians.

She looked up and stared straight at the chief. She turned and brushed by him as she entered her house and closed the door. Once inside, Nancy leaned against the door. A wave of feelings came over her. Tears ran down her face as she thought about her dead husband. "Those damn Indians," she thought. "They killed my husband and they have my son. I don't even know if he is alive or dead. It's time for me to stop pretending with these savages. I want my son back. I want a new life with Thomas and my son," Nancy ended.

She walked into the living room and started to keep herself busy with cleaning and rearranging what was left of the furniture. She worked for hours until she grew hungry. She went into the kitchen and started to make herself something to eat when she heard a noise at the back door. She glanced around the room and in the corner was the spear. Nancy grabbed it up and stood behind the door and waited. When the door opened, it was the chief. She yelled and lunged forward. Just missing him and impaling the spear into the wall. Her eyes locked with the chief and they just stood there. Nancy was holding the spear at one end and the chief's holding the other.

"You don't have to worry about anyone hurting you Nancy. No one here will do that," The chief said.

"Really, how can I believe that? How can I believe that from someone that killed my husband and stole my son? From someone that left hundreds of people with nothing but death. You took everything that we had, things that can never be replaced. I hate you for that. I hate your people for what they have done," Nancy ended.

"You speak the truth Nancy, but I want you to talk to my father. I will bring him here as the sun sets high above us. Just talk to him, will you Nancy?" The chief ended.

"Talk to your father? Why are you afraid of a woman? You have to have your father talk for you?" Nancy said.

The chief pulled the spear out of the wall and out of Nancy's hands. "My father is wise. His words flow better than mine. We will be here," the chief walked out the door carrying the spear.

Nancy fell onto the table and buried her face in her hands. She hoped that Thomas would hurry up and get back to her. She sat up and went back to making her meal. All that morning she kept herself busy, going from room to room cleaning and getting everything in order. As she cleaned her last window, she noticed the sun was almost above her. She gathered herself up and walked to the kitchen. She sat herself at the table and waited. She was lighting candles when she heard someone on the back porch. The door opened and in walked the chief and an old man. The old man stopped and looked at the hole in the wall and said something to his son.

"What is he saying?" Nancy asked.

"He said that he should have given you a different name. He says you have spirit," the chief.

The old man started talking to the chief. "He says you must listen to all he has to say before you speak. Do you understand? I will interpret for him what he says, word, for word."

"Yes, fine. But I will have the last say this day," Nancy said as she sat back down.

The old man starts to talk, looking into Nancy's eyes as he spoke.

"When I was a boy, my grandfather came to me and said we must go for a walk. We walked deep into the woods and sat upon a hickory log. He talked about the days of his youth, the days of many buffalo, and the days of few white men. I had never seen a white man before and I was curious about them and their ways. My grandfather talked about how at first they were nice and how they helped each other. The white man started to build on Indian land. They started to take land that was only owned by the Great Father. They took the sacred burial land of our pasted fathers and mothers. The years pasted and the white man crawled across this land like ants from a hill. They devoured everything in their path. They killed our men, women and children; burned our villages and took all the buffalo. They took everything we worked for. They changed our way of life. We once were a proud people. We lived our lives with peace to each other and nature. The white man changed this. They forced us to fight against each other. Indian fought Indian. Our lands ran red with Indian blood. My mother was killed when our village was burned to the ground. I have buried my father, mother, sister and brothers. You have lost, yes, but we have lost many times over. No one owns this land. How can you own the wind? How can you own the heart of nature? This land is free from everyone, including the white man. The times of Indians living free are few. The white man wants to put us into large villages, living like animals. There is no respect in that. Our way of life is over; we live from one sun to the next. We teach our young the ways of days gone by. We sing for the dead and pray for the living."

The old man stopped talking and Nancy just looked at him. Then she spoke.

"I am sorry for your loss. I understand you didn't ask for this, but I didn't do this to you. If I could go back and change things, I would. I would give back everything that you lost, everything that you held deep in your heart. I would give this to you," Nancy started to cry. "You said that I had lost. Yes I did. Your men killed my husband and stole my son. I need my son..." Nancy laid her hands on the old mans hand. "I need my son!" Nancy cried.

The old man waved his other hand at the chief. The chief opened the door and then in walked a young brave. He was dressed in ragged clothes and was dirty. Nancy stood up and slowly walked over to the boy. He was white.

"Kyle?" Nancy asks.

The boy looked up with a questioned look on his face.

"Kyle. Is it you? Do you remember me?"

The little boy looked at the old man and the old man spoke to him. He walked closer to Nancy and spoke.

"My name is David. David Stevens but I knew a Kyle. He was taken by the Blackfoot Indians a few months ago. A few of us boys were fishing when they rode down on us. They took Kyle and another boy named Mike. We ran into the woods. Hours later when we returned to the village Kyle and Mike didn't show. I'm sorry," the boy ended and spoke to the old man, then walked out the door.

"The Blackfoot will take good care of your boy. They will treat him like their own. With him being white, if the soldiers come they will return him. I hope this can rest your heart," the old man said as he left. The chief sat quietly as he looked at Nancy. "You will see him again but just not right away. Keep his thoughts with you everyday. One day he will return," then the chief left also.

Nancy's head was spinning. Anyway she looked at it her son was still with Indians and she still didn't know if he was dead or alive. That evening she tried to keep her wits about her. She went to some of the other houses and gathered supplies for her house. She took old glass from windows and replaced her broken ones. While she looked though each house, she would stop and browse the pictures and clothing, remembering each person who had lived there. The houses were still in really good shape and with a little fixing up this town could thrive again.

As she was finishing the window in her bedroom she noticed a piece of paper sticking out from under her pillow. Nancy crossed to the bed and lay down. She took out the paper.

It was a note from Thomas.

"Nancy...

When you find this note I will have left on our journey. I will return to you, my love, but until I do, look under my pillow. I bought this for you from Mole. He drives a hard bargain, but you are worth every penny. Until I see you keep this near you heart.

Love always, Thomas"

Nancy slid her hand under Thomas's pillow and took out a small box. When she opened it, it took her by surprise. It was the cameo necklace. She held it out in front of her as her eyes teared up. She placed it around her neck. "I will never take this off, Thomas. I promise," she said as she looked out the window. The sun was almost gone as the darkness of the night entered the small town. Nancy hurried down stairs and placed chairs against all the doors to keep everyone out. She went back upstairs and blew out the candles and lay upon Thomas's pillow holding her necklace.

"Good night, Thomas," She said as she fell sleep.

Nancy slept though the night for the first time in a while. She was only awakened by a loud clap of thunder. It was daylight outside. She was caught between going back to sleep and getting up for the day. She felt the sunlight hitting her face. In the distance of her mind, she could hear someone blowing a horn. Then she could hear the sound of running horses, lots of horses. She sat up and looked out her window. What she saw made her skin crawl. It was the Calvary charging into town. The horn sounds got closer until she could see a few hundred men riding hard. In the back of them were wagons. She couldn't see the end of the line.

"My God... The Army!" Nancy thought.

She sprang up and started to dress herself. She could hear them on her front porch. The men were yelling and she could hear them pounding on her door. She ran downstairs and swung open the front door. She watched as a few men dismounted and started to go through the buildings of the town. One man on a large horse just sat there smiling at Nancy. Another man came running up to him.

"Sir, there seems to be no one here but this white woman. No Indians," He said as he pointed at Nancy.

As the man got off his horse he took off his hat and came to the front of the porch.

"Private, I'm sure that this white woman, as you put it, has a name?" He said as he smiled at Nancy.

"Ma'am, I'm lit. Colonel Mitchell, Dan Mitchell. May I ask... what the hell are you doing here?" the Colonel questioned.

I'm Nancy Bach. This is my home. I live here. Why do you asked?" Nancy said.

"Well, our information says that a band of Crow Indians are living in this town. Mrs. Bach is your husband home?"

"No, he is off to Helena getting supplies. He should be back in a week. Would you like some coffee, Colonel?" Nancy asked.

"Yes, I would. It would give us time to talk. Private, get the men and set up camp. Send out a hunting party and take inventory on our supplies. If we are low, send out a small party to Helena and get what we need. I need everything set up before noon." The Colonel gestured with his hand to the front door for Nancy to pass.

"Yes sir, by noon," The private said running off.

Nancy turned and entered the house. The Colonel watched and

Nancy built a fire and set the coffee pot on the stove.

"Okay Mrs. Bach, how long have you been living here? The Colonel asked.

Well, my first husband built this house about eight years ago. He was killed when the Crow took over this town. I've been back here for about three weeks. Haven't seen any Indians. Maybe they moved on," Nancy lied.

"But our reports indicate that the Crow are here and they have been here living in this area. It is my orders to pursue and capture these renegade Indians and take them to the holding stations, to be processed," The Colonel ended.

"Well, if they are here, why can't you just leave them alone? Why can't you just let them live out their lives, like they have been for generations?"

Ma'am, they are the last of the renegade Crow. They will continue to kill and steal, until their last dying breath."

Nancy stood up and got the hot coffee and poured it into two cups.

"Thank you. Actually, I really can't see many of them surviving the attack. Once we locate where the have set up camp. I foresee only a few living through that. We will camp here for a few days until we get our updated supplies. In the meantime we will send out scouts, Indian scouts, to cover this area. Mrs. Bach, don't worry now that we are here, we will pursue them and if we don't find anything, we will move on. I will leave a few men here to protect you until your husband returns," The Cornel said as he drank his coffee.

"I don't need protected. I just need left alone!" Nancy said.

"It is my duty to protect the fine people of this great nation. You really have no say in this matter. The Army does what the Army sees fit. If I wanted, I could just burn down this town. That way there would be no reason for either the Crow or us to be here. Is that what you want? Because if it is I can surely do this. Then I could move on to Helena myself, maybe even get a bath. You know, relax for a while." The Cornel said smiling as he set down his cup of coffee.

"Well, you can leave whatever men you want, but I do not want anything to do with them. You, Colonel, as well as your men are to leave me alone. Do we understand each other? And when my husband returns, he can discuss it further with you. Now, I have work to do." (Nancy went to the kitchen back door and opens it) 'If you don't mind, you have worn out your welcome," Nancy exclaimed.

The Colonel stood up, placing his hat on his head. He tipped his hat to Nancy and left through the backdoor. Nancy closed the door and placed a chair under the handle. She then went upstairs and peered out her bedroom window. She watched as they set up in the empty houses. The Colonel set up is headquarters in the saloon. There were so many men running around to town. They were like the old Indian had said, "*Like ants running a crossed the land.* "

After a few hours of watching the men, Nancy started her chores. Gathering supplies like candles, materials and anything of worth. She gathered water. She tried to keep her mind busy and tried to ignore the men that followed her. They watched her every move. It wasn't until the late afternoon that she realized that she hadn't eaten all day. She ate biscuit and gravy for a late supper. She cleaned up and once again placed chairs on all the doors. She lit her candle and entered her bedroom. As she walked into the room, she saw a shadow on the wall. A large shadow of a man.

"Don't move. I have a gun! Who are you and what do you want?" Nancy exclaimed.

The shadow slowly crossed the room, the light shown upon the face. It was the Chief.

"Why are those men here?" He asked.

"They are looking for you and your people," Nancy said.

"What have you told them?"

"Nothing. I just said I haven't seen any Indians but they will find you. And the Colonel said that they will take the survivors to camps. You must go and hide. They will leave in a few days, only leaving a few men here to watch over me," Nancy ended.

"They will find us. They will not leave so easily. I will leave with the ones that want to go. The strong men and young braves. Some will stay—the very young and the old will stay and be found. It will be the only way our people will roam this land again free and wild. When you husband returns, tell him that we are going to Elkhorn. He is to meet us at the Sabathia, the arrow rock. We will camp there for 30 suns. After that we will be hunting for him. Tell him that we will want our share of the money. I expect no less from him. He is our friend and we will not hurt him, but we will need money to live out the winter in the mountains. Take care Nancy Bach. It is a sad day for my people. Please remember me and my braves as good strong people. Don't let the white man sway your ideas of us," The Chief said and he hurried through the door.

Nancy sat on her bed and watched as the sun set. She hoped that the Indians would be safe, but deep in her heart she knew that their lives would be over. The army would slaughter all the men and the young and old would live out their lives in a camp.

"With this no one wins," Nancy thought.

She watched the Army men all that week. There was still no signs of Thomas and she didn't seen any Indians being brought into camp, until the 7th day. When Nancy awoke that morning, she could hear sounds of laughter and men yelling. She looked out her window and saw men pushing and kicking a large group of Indians down Main Street. Their hands were tied and they looked weak and pale. As they were paraded past her window she saw the young children. It was at this time that she heard a pounding on her front door. She dressed quickly and raced down the stairs. When she opened the door standing in front of her, were five white children. Standing behind them was the Colonel.

"Mrs. Bach we have located the camp of the Crow. All we could find were the old and the children. The few Indians that speak English tell me that the Chief and the young braves have all left, not to return. We also found these white children. They speak English. We were hoping that you would take care of them for a while until we could get this straightened out. If not we will have to put them with the others and place them into camps," The Colonel ended.

Nancy stood silent for a moment and just looked at the children. Three girls and two boys, but she did not see her son.

"Well of course I'll take then in, but I'll need food and supplies. These children are from our town. They will stay here without any hindrance from you or your Army. Do I make myself clear?" With that she guided the children into the house down the main hall, looking back over her shoulder at the Colonel. "Food and supplies should be taken to the back door and you should be ashamed of yourself for what you are doing to those people! They just want left alone to live their lives."

"Just following orders ma'am. You'll get your supplies, Mrs. Bach, but please keep your comments to yourself or I'll have to arrest you as an Indian sympathizer. And that wouldn't be good," The colonel threatened.

Nancy slammed the door in his face. She turned and faced the children. They looked scared and lonely.

"Well now my name is Mrs. Bach. I live here and so shall you. Please step forward and tell me your name and who your parents were, if you can remember, girls first."

The first girl stepped up. "I'm Mary. I'm, 11 years old and I don't know who my parents were."

"Well it is nice to meet you, Mary. Welcome."

The next little girl stepped up but didn't say anything. Mary spoke up. "She only speaks Crow. I think she is 4 or so. I'm not really sure. She lived with the Chief's children and mother," Mary said.

The last girl walked up. "I'm Janet Walton. I'm 14 and I do remember you. You had a son, Kyle…that lived with us, but your husband was kill in the attack. Your last name used to be… Riley? Was that your name before?" Janet asked.

"Yes, it was, but I have now remarried a fine man named Thomas Bach. So, it is Mrs. Bach."

The boys walked up. "I'm David, David Stevens. I'm 13 years old and my mother and father owned the grainery on the edge of town. I also knew Kyle. He was taken by the Blackfoot Indians. Me and Kyle would come back into town and we would come to this house. He took your picture from the fireplace. He always wanted to find you. This is my little brother, Taylor. He is 5 and he doesn't talk much."

Nancy looked at the children.

"First things first. Boys, I want you to grab the water buckets from the back porch and bring water to the stove. In the mean time the girls and I will go and so what clothes we can find," Nancy stated.

Nancy stoked the fire in the stove and placed wood into it. The boys placed water into the pots.

"Now while we are gone, I want you boys to wash up. Just pour the water into the bathtub. We should be gone for just a little while. I would take separate baths. Your really dirty," Nancy joked as she and the girls left.

As Nancy and the girls crossed the street to the main part of town, Mary spoke up.

"I have always had a feeling about this house. Mrs. Bach do you think that this could be my old house?"

"I don't know, but lets go in." Nancy and the girls walked into the house. As they stepped into the large family room, Mary saw pictures on the fireplace mantel.

"This house belonged to the Rev. Fletcher," Nancy said.

Mary took down one of the photos and wiped the dust off of it. In the photo was the Rev. and a woman holding a small child. Mary slid the photo from the frame. On the back of this photo written in large letters was, "*Mary Margaret Fletcher.*"

"Mary this is your home. These are photos of your parents." Nancy said.

Mary just stood there studying the faces of the man and the woman in the photo.

In a low voice Mary said, "I still don't remember them. But I remember this house."

"That's okay sweetie. We'll take the photos with us so you can have them. Maybe after a while your memory will come back." Nancy said.

Nancy climbed the stairs with the girls following right behind her. They searched every room. Then they came to the master bedroom. When they looked in the closet, they found a very large trunk. Nancy dragged the trunk out to the center of the room. The big buckles were rusted closed. Nancy used a piece of wood from the broken window to pry open the first buckle. After all the buckles were opened the girls opened the trunk. The trunk was filled with Mary's mother's dresses. The girls went touched each dress and Nancy knew that she could alter the dresses to fit Mary, but what about the other girls? The group searched the remaining houses and managed to find clothes for the other children. They were not the best, but they would do for now.

The girls and Nancy entered Nancy's home through the kitchen. The boys were bathed and sitting at the table with their old clothes on.

"Boys, now go through these clothes and find something that is close to fitting for now. I'll adjust then later. Now, girls go get your bath." Nancy ended.

As the boys entered the kitchen once again wearing the new clothes, Nancy could tell that the clothes were a little big. Nancy handed them some rope.

"Now, one last thing. Please sit down and get your first hair cut in a long time. David, you're first," Nancy ended.

Nancy took out a bowl and placed it on David's head and cut along the edges. The hair hit the floor in a big pile. With a little more cutting, David was now looking like a young man again. Taylor stood and watched as his brother got his haircut.

"Come on Taylor. It's your turn." David said as he brushed off the hair from his shoulders. Taylor just looked at the hair pile and slowly climbed onto the chair. Nancy started cutting his hair. All the while the young boy stared at her. Nancy just smiled and said,

"I do believe that their maybe a young man under this bush of hair. Don't worry your going to look good when I'm done. Just like your brother."

Taylor just looked at his brother and rolled his eyes. Nancy and David laughed at the way Taylor acted.

"There, were done," Nancy said.

As Nancy finished with Taylor, she saw out of the corner of her eye the 3 girls standing at the doorway. They had managed to find clothes that almost fit.

"O.K. kids line up for inspection. David and Taylor you're looking good, a hundred times better," Nancy said as she took her thumb and wiped David's forehead, "But you missed a spot. Janet, Mary and....and my dear, what are we going to call you?" Nancy said as she knelt down to the littlest girl. Nancy thought for a moment.

"How about Laura May. That was my mother's name. I think that it will fit you. How does that sound, Laura May?"

The child didn't say anything. She just stood there and looked into Nancy's eyes. Then she nodded up and down.

"Great! Then Laura is it! Now let's clean up this mess and start lunch."

The children carried in the supplies that the Army left. Nancy noticed that they had a lot of flour but not much meat. She would have to talk to the Colonel about this. She made lunch for the children-biscuits and gravy, again.

Nancy thought "How will I feed these children on just flour and a few mixes?"

She just hoped that Thomas would return soon. As the children ate, she stared out the window and thought about Thomas. It had been ten days since he left. With every day that passed, her hopes for his return lessens. Thomas had told her that it would only be a few days, maybe a week, but would he be back? Would he be back in time, now that Nancy has all these mouths to feed?

"Mrs. Bach...Mrs. Bach..." David asked "Are you all right?"

"Yes. Yes. David my mind was just wondering. I'm fine. I have a wonderful idea for this afternoon. Lets go to the river and do some fishing for supper. I have some old nets and string. I'll pack us a snack and we can talk. How does that sound?" Nancy asked.

Janet and David looked at each other. "That sounds great Mrs. Bach."

As the children gathered the supplies, Nancy had another idea. In the morning the children and she were going to go to the old schoolhouse and see what was left. She would start teaching the kids as soon as possible.

Nancy and the children walked down the path to the river that was behind Nancy's home. Nancy noticed a drastic change in the children, not only their appearance, but also in their attitude. When they first came, they had seemed distant, answering questions with one word and speaking only when they were told to. Now, after only a few hours they seemed more open. They were talking to each other as they walked down the path. As they approached the river bank, David layed out the net and Janet and the girls looked for worms.

It was then that Nancy noticed berries-Blackberries, blue-berries.

"Laura May, Mary, and Janet come with me. Here, let's use our baskets and fill it full of berries. Laura May, Mary you pick these blackberries and Janet and I will pick the blueberries. Let's fill the baskets and tomorrow I'll make pies."

The boys started to fish off the banks. Taylor used the worms that they found and David tried to use the net. David flung the net out to the deepest part of the river. On David's first pull from the river, the net was empty. He moved down a little further and again...nothing.

"Mrs. Bach, I'm thinking that this river may be fished out. The crow fished this river heavy down stream." David said.

"Try casting your net under the overhanging tree branches. My dad always told me that fish like to swim in the shade during the heat of the day," Nancy explained.

David waded in to his knees and flung the net again, only this time he threw it into the tree branches. Nancy and the other children busted out laughing.

"Looks like you need a little practice. You'll have to cross the river and untangle your net," Nancy said.

Nancy looked around at the children laughing at David, even the younger ones were smiling and laughing. How happy they seemed. David set out to untangle his net when Nancy started asking questions.

"Janet, what was it like living with the Crow? Were they good to you?" Nancy asked.

"Well, the first month was the hardest. All the children wanted to go home. They didn't understand what happened to them. The older kids that were 15 and older were put to work bring in water, wood cutting, all the heavy work. I had to help the Chiefs wife. She taught me to tan hides, cut meat and cook," Janet said.

"Well, we do have something in common. Remind me to show you my bear hide," Nancy said.

"Life was hard. After a year, we soon realized that we weren't coming home and that we wouldn't see any of our parents or friends again. It was about this time that we were allowed to come back to town for short visits. After a time it was all just a memory-like that old way of life never existed. Almost like a dream. Then last week the Chief made an announcement to his people. He said the strong braves and him were moving on to another place. That they could no longer feed his village. That the children and the old should turn themselves in to the Army and live out their days on white mans land. If he and the braves stayed, they would be killed and that this would solve nothing. That night they danced, sang and in the morning left camp. In the afternoon, the elders gathered wood for a large fire and lit it. I guess the Army saw the smoke. They found us and took us into town and here we are. Back home, back to where it all began," Janet ended.

"But now you are here we can start over, a fresh start, but I'll need your help with the other children. We will work together to build this town back to what it once was," Nancy ended.

"That would be nice," Janet agreed.

Just then everyone heard a large splashing noise coming from the river's edge.

"Where is David?" Nancy yelled.

Nancy and the children ran to the river bank, just in time to see David throw up one very large catfish onto the bank.

"It's huge," Mary said.

"It's gotta be at least 20 pounds!" David exclaimed.

"It's a big fish," Laura said.

Everyone now looked at Laura. It was the first words she had spoken all day. Nancy gathered her up and hugged her.

"Laura you can talk. That's wonderful!" Nancy said.

"Great now we can have supper. How is the berry picking going girls?" Nancy asked.

"The baskets are almost full," Mary stated.

"O.K. Everyone pick berries. We have enough fish for today. Great job everyone! So if we work as a group we can get things done. Now back to the house," Nancy said.

As Nancy opened the back door, the Colonel was sitting at the table.

"Hey the kids look great and look you have supper!" The Colonel exclaimed.

"Children please put away all the nets and line. Wash up and come back and help with supper." Nancy then turned to the Cornel. "May I help you Colonel?"

"Well Mrs. Bach we have word from one of the Crow elders that the Chief has left them for dead. He has taken his braves and left the weak and young. I will be leaving in the morning with most of my men to pursue these braves. In the meantime, I would like you to continue your mothering of the white children and upon our return in a week or so, we will have to take them to Helena to the Priest to be raised by the word of God. They have lived with the devil for years, they need church to bring them back to God. Do we understand each other, Mrs. Bach?" The Colonel ended.

"The white children? What kind of a man are you? The church of God? Yes, they need that, but they also need to stay here. To stay in the only family they have left. You sit there sporting orders. You have no idea what you are talking about when it comes to these children. In one day, in just one day they have started coming out of their shells. Just starting to laugh again. In the morning, I plan on reopening the old school house, fixing what needs fixed and starting the schooling as soon as possible. This point in time, I'm sure God will understand if it takes a few days before they attend church but that will come. While I'm at it, you say you'll be returning in a week, to ten days, to take the children. Well, I have news for you! You had better bring more men than you have right now, because you'll need them to get these children out of this house. Now, leave this house Colonel and take your kill first, ask questions later attitude with you!" Nancy ended as she slammed her fist down on the table.

"Are you done, Mrs. Bach?" The Cornel asked.

"Yes, quite done, Colonel."

"Again, I'm just following orders. Orders that come from very high up. But if you can get this ragged old town up and running again, I can inform the powers that be… and maybe the kids—I mean children would be better off left here. But I do have one last question for you. Do you know where the Crow have gone?" There was a long silence as the Colonel looked at Nancy. "It has come to my attention, also though one of the elders, that you have talked to and are currently talking to the Chief. What do you say about that Mrs. Bach?"

"That's the stupidest thing that I have ever heard and the answer is no, Colonel, But try and have a good week of Indian chasing." Nancy said as she handed the Colonel his hat.

"Have a good evening Ma'am. But if you would talk to the Chief, just by accident, tell him that I am going to find his band and kill him. Tell him I will hang his head on the end of a spear and show it to his people. Do you understand me Mrs. Bach?" The Colonel said smiling and tipping his hat while he walk out the door.

Nancy closed the door and leaned her back against it. She could hear the children laughing and then they came running into the kitchen.

"Thank you, Mrs. Bach." Janet said.

"We need not worry ourselves about anything at this point. Janet, Mary Laura, did you see any sugar in the supplies left by the Army?" Nancy asked

"No, we didn't, but we didn't look at everything," Janet said.

"David, Taylor, go first to the Colonel and ask him for some sugar. Then I'll need you to bring in water for supper." Nancy stated.

Yes, ma'am," the boys were quick to agree.

"Girls let's clean that fish and get a fire started," Nancy smiled.

Everyone set out on their jobs. Nancy watched the children work and started the fire in the stove. Taylor came in the kitchen running.

"This is all they would give us, Mrs. Bach," Taylor said holding up a small bag.

"Taylor, I see you are talking also. You have a wonderful voice. This should be enough sugar. Now,go help David with the water," Nancy said.

"Do you want the fish cut up for drying or frying?" Janet asked.

"Frying...I'm not eating dried fish," Mary laughed.

The boys returned with the water. Nancy made her pies. As the children worked, Nancy went upstairs to see where everyone would sleep. She would give her son's room to the boys and the girls could sleep in the big bedroom next to the boys. She laid out blankets on the beds. As she was coming down the stairs, she could smell supper cooking. Nancy entered the kitchen and saw Janet, Mary and Laura standing beside the stove.

"What a wonderful smell," Nancy exclaimed.

"We are having fried fish, fried potatoes and mushrooms and the pies look like they need a few more minutes," Mary said.

"Pie, blueberry pie," Laura sighed.

Nancy set the table as the children served her. As the last plate was set on the table the children sat down. Mary held out her hands and everyone joined hands with heads bowed.

"Oh, heavenly Father, we want to thank you for this bounty of food that you have provided for us. May it nourish these children. I would also like to thank you for letting us find each other. May you help keep us together. In Jesus name. Amen," Nancy prayed.

The new family ate all the dinner and then Nancy took the children to their rooms.

They were told to get ready for bed. The sun had been down for a few hours and the chill of the night we starting. Nancy tucked in all of the children. She said her good nights and she went to her room. How dark and lonely it seemed without Thomas. She sat on her bed looking out the window. The army had a large fire going. Nancy held her necklace tight against her chest. "Thomas hurry home. I have a surprise for you. I see my moon is shining bright. Find your way back to me, Thomas Bach. Find your way back!"

Nancy slid into bed and as her head hit the pillow, she could hear a small knock on her door. It was Laura.

"I'm scared, Mrs. Bach. May I sleep with you tonight? Just for tonight." Laura asked.

"Why sure Laura, but just for tonight." Nancy said.

Laura jumped into bed and held Nancy as she blew out the candle.

Nancy thought, "Hurry back, Thomas. Find your way back to me."

Chapter Seven
"The Heart of the Arrow"

Thomas and the braves crossed back around to Arrow Rock.

"All right Wolf, we're here. Now where's the heart of the arrow? We have to go North West at 315' from the heart. We only have about an hour 'til sunset," Thomas said.

"Legend has it that the heart of the Sabathia arrow can only be seen on the first morning light. We will camp here for the night. We will rest Thomas Bach, 'til morning's first light. Then the heart will be revealed to us," Wolf explained.

The men made camp and Puma had a long talk with Wolf. Then he gathered his belonging and left at almost sunset. Thomas and the braves made beds in the wagon, using what they could as covers. They couldn't afford to have a fire, lest someone would see their location.

Thomas sat to the front of the wagon looking at the stars as they came out one at a time. A full moon shone down upon the mountain. Thomas was just about to doze off when he heard a noise in the woods. "Is it Puma returning?" he thought. He slowly grabbed his colt and eased it up. With the moon he should be able to see who was coming through the woods. There walking toward the wagon was a large bull elk. He was grazing on acorns. Thomas smiled and was so involved in watching the animal that it didn't dawn on him to kill it. Thomas heard the sound of rushing air. The elk staggered and fell to his side.

"What...Wolf someone just killed an elk in front of the wagon...Wolf?" Thomas couldn't find Wolf.

"Yes, Thomas, it was me," Wolf said, "The Great Spirit has given us meat for our journey. Red Fox, help me cut up this elk."

"Wolf, has Puma returned? Where has he gone?" Thomas asked.

"Puma has gone back to town to inform our father of our change in plans. It will be just the three of us from here on out. They will meet us back here in 2 days," Wolf ended.

Thomas sat back down in the wagon and laid his head on the floor. He thought that Puma's leaving was not a good thing because they really needed him in case of attack. His thoughts soon turned to dreams. As Thomas slept, the braves worked on the elk and then they too fell asleep beside the wagon.

Thomas awoke just as the light was starting to climb over the ridge. He climbed out of the wagon just to see Wolf and Red Fox standing in front of the Arrow Rock. Then just as the red sunlight hit the rock, in the upper right corner a large outcrop of the rock could be seen. It was the first part of the rock to get the light.

"Here is your heart, Thomas Bach," Wolf said.

Thomas got out his compass and pointed it to northwest 315'. He raised his scope and started to scan the mountain range. Slowly he covered the mountain looking for a sign or clue.

"The heart of the rock, see the graves of friends...MAF." Thomas thought to himself.

"Nothing...I see nothing but woods," Thomas said.

"206 chains, Thomas Bach, we have to have a starting point," Wolf warned.

Thomas then scanned from the river up. About half way up the mountain he could see a clearing. "Why would there be a clearing there? The woods cover completely around the mountain," He thought.

Then he saw it. He saw the corner of a roof of a house or shed. "I see something. It's the roof of a house or shed. We must cross the river to get there. I'm sure you can see the rock from there. Where can we cross the river?" Thomas asked

"Down river about 2 miles. It is shallow, but it is also open. To cross that part it must be done at night. It would be dangerous to cross during the daylight," Wolf ended.

"So be it then. Let's cross around and over. These wagons will only go so far, then the horses will have to be used. I don't really like losing another day, but if it is the only way. Don't forget Wolf, good thing's come to those that wait." Thomas quoted.

"Yes, but if we wait too long, no good thing will come but the Siksika," Wolf said.

Slowly the three crossed back over and down the side of the mountain. Until they came to a road divided. Thomas stopped the wagon and looked at Wolf.

"Well, which way now?" Thomas asked.

"I will take this road to see if it goes to the river. Red Fox stay here with Bach. If I am not back after a short time, hide the wagons, ride only in the woods not the road," Wolf ended.

Wolf took his horse and rode along the woodline down the road. Now Thomas and Red Fox just looked at each other.

"So, Red Fox, you are the youngest of the three brothers?"

"Quiet Bach! My father told me to protect you but I don't have to listen to you. And if this whole thing is a lie, I will be the one who kills you, now silence." Red Fox threatened.

Thomas sat for a while and then he smelled this weird smell coming from his wagon. He turned and looked into the back and he found the reason for the smell. Wolf and Red Fox had cut the elk into long thin strips of meat. They laid them out on the floor of the wagon, blood was everywhere. The blood had even drained into the bag of biscuits.

"What is this Red Fox?" Thomas demanded.

"The meat is drying. We will have to hang it soon. As soon as the blood finishes dripping from the meat," Red Fox explained.

"Yes, but look at the mess in my wagon. Plus the flies are everywhere and I guess this is our supper?" Thomas ended.

Red Fox just shook his head at Thomas. "Don't worry, it will not kill you." Red Fox said.

"No, that's your job, right?" Thomas said drolly.

Thomas got down from the wagon to stretched out his back. He looked down the road and in the distance he could see Wolf riding hard.

"Wolf is coming."

"We must hurry. The Siksika are close. We must take the wagons and hide them in the thick brush. Take only what we need. This is the road to the river, but there are many horse tracks, fresh tracks. We must be fast," Wolf stated.

The men pushed the wagons into the brush and placed bushes on top to hide them completely. They took the horses and started back down the road to the river. The dirt road was rough and soon turned into just a path, with thick brush and trees on both sides. They went down a steep hill. It was then that Thomas could hear the river. The men stopped about twenty feet from the edge of the woods. Thomas took out his scope and looked at the water. It was shallow, only about a foot deep.

"Now, we must wait for dark," Wolf said.

"Wouldn't it be better if we waited until almost sunrise, crossed in the dark, then as the sun rose we would have light to see?" Thomas questioned

"That would be good. Red Fox let's eat and then rest. No fires." Wolf said.

The men ate dry biscuits and meat and water. "Lunch fit for a king, but I guess it is better than nothing." Thomas ended.

"You have lived the good life too long Thomas Bach. Once we have crossed back safely into Crow lands, we will have a Chief's feast," Wolf said.

"I'm sorry I just hate waiting around. I know it is for the best, but I worry about Nancy. I told her a week to ten days, now it has taken us that long just to get this far. It may take ten more days until we reach home," Thomas worried.

"The Chief will not allow anything to happen to her. She will be safe. We must not worry about anything, Thomas Bach. I have a good feeling about this journey. We must be smart and not leave any sign that we were here. The Great Spirit will protect us from our enemies. Let us rest now, in the morning we will need our strength to follow us to the clearing," Wolf said as he sat down to eat.

Thomas laid down and put his head against a sod of grass. He ate some flat meat from his pocket and watched the sunlight glisten off the water.

The next thing he remembered was waking up to someone calling his name.

"Bach, we must go now." Wolf said, "We will lead our horses across the river, then ride up stream to the clearing."

Thomas grabbed the reins of his horse and slowly they waded across the river. The moon danced off the water as they walked. Ever so slowly the group meandered forward, with Wolf leading the way. After all three crossed, they mounted their horses and rode along the river bank. As they rode the sun started to peak over the hill. They rode until they came upon the clearing.

"Now we must wait for the sunlight to show us the way." Wolf said.

As the light reached the valley Thomas could see the clearing and an old house. Thomas turned and looked behind and he could see the rock. It took all the horses had to climb up the steep hill. Small rocks made the horses slip and slide up and back. When they reached a log house, the three men got a clear picture of everything. Tall grass had taken over the fields and mixed in with the grass were small trees starting to shoot upward. The house had one side that had almost collapsed down. They were no signs of life anywhere.

"This place has no life. Even the birds do not sing here," Wolf said.

Thomas dismounted and walked to the open door. As he pushed the door completely open, he could see something laying on the floor. As he walked closer he noticed they were skeletons.

"We have bodies in here. They have been dead for awhile. Not much left but bones," Thomas explained.

Wolf walked over and picked up something off the floor. "An arrow, Siksika arrow.

Looks like man and woman." Wolf stated.

Thomas began to examine the room. He noticed a large book sitting on the table. It was a diary. Written on the cover was *Rev. Donald P. Friend and wife, Dorothy Ellen Friend.* Thomas read out loud. The first few pages talked about how they had come here to set up a mission for the Indians and do God's work. The pages went on to explain how they had befriended the Indians and how they helped each other. Then the diary just stopped.

"They stopped writing in the diary over a year and a half ago. I wonder what happened?"

"The Siksika must have wanted something. Killing for them means nothing," Wolf said.

I guess they were missionaries. Spreading the word of God," Thomas said.

"More white people trying to change us. Trying to make us what we are not. I guess they did not change the Siksika," Wolf ended.

Thomas placed the book back on the table and looked out the back window. Something was sticking up over top of the tall grass. It was a large rock. "Too smooth to be an outcrop," Thomas thought.

He walked to the rock and pushed the grass down. There was some writing. Thomas cleaned off the rock with his hand. Thomas could make out the letters… "James." He thought for a minute and then stood up and yelled, "It's a grave!"

Wolf and Red fox came running to Thomas's side.

"Quick, look for more and clean off the stones so we can read the names," Thomas exclaimed.

The three worked and pushed the tall grass down and found five more headstones.

"Can you read any of this?" Thomas asked.

"Not yet, but I do have a last name. Friend, it looks like Friend," Wolf said.

Thomas fell back and sat down and started laughing.

"What is so funny, Bach?" Red Fox asked.

"Don't you get it, The graves of Friends. On the map it says the graves of friends." Thomas took out the map and read it out loud. "The grave of friends… quick look for someone with the initials of M.A.F." They cleaned off all the stones but no M.A.F. "I don't understand this, it's has to be here." Thomas said as he sat back down. Then peeking out of the grass, he saw another rock that was under a large oak tree.

"Here, check here," Thomas pointed.

Wolf and Red Fox followed Thomas to the large stone. Carefully they wiped the front of the headstone off and in big bold letters was the name, "Marshall Allen Friend."

"This is it—M.A.F. Hurry start digging!" The three men worked for over an hour until they came upon a large steel box. They couldn't lift the box out of the grave. It was stuck in the ground.

"It's stuck in the soil. What are we going to do Thomas Bach? We can't move it," Wolf complained.

"Just watch." With that Thomas took the shovel and slammed it down hard against the side of the box. One of the hinges broke off. He struck it again and again until the other side broke. Then he pried the lid to one side. "Now it's open," Thomas said.

The three men looked down into the hole, then they looked at each other. It was a beautiful site, shining in the sun. Thomas and the braves were grinning form ear to ear; they had found the treasure.

"Well, fellas, are you just gonna sit there, or are you going to get the bags and load up?" Thomas asked.

They took burlap bags and started to place both gold coins and paper money into them. The bags were heavy and they tied them together and laid them across the horses shoulders.

"We will do like the Chief said. We will count it when we get back to town, but not until then," Thomas said.

Thomas then looked to the sky, "Regan, you old friend, I believed in you. I believed in you even when I had my doubts. Thank you."

"We must go now. We must cross the river and head for the wagon," Wolf ordered.

"But it is daylight. Should we wait for dark?" Thomas asked.

"We have waited long enough. We have gotten what we came for. Now we must get back to town," Wolf stated.

The men rode hard along the wood's edge, following the river bank until they came to the crossing. Thomas got out his scope and looked to the other side.

"It looks clear; should we cross?"

"We cannot wait 'til dark. It will not be dark for hours. We could be out of Siksika land in that time. We cross now," Wolf said as he took off across the river.

Red Fox and Thomas followed. As they neared the river bank, Thomas looked though his scope along the bank, then up the path. He saw a movement in the brush. It was an Indian. A young brave, that jumped on his horse and rode up the path.

Wolf looked up the trail and saw the young brave riding up the path. "A scout—we must push on. He is too young to be a brave, but we must hurry. He will warn others, Bach I must tell you something," Wolf said.

"What is it?" Thomas asked.

"The Siksika have this boy named Kyle. The boy that you and Nancy seek is in the Siksika village. Father didn't want me to tell you till later," Wolf said.

"Kyle? They have Kyle. We'll talk about this later Wolf," Thomas said.

The three rode hard up the steep trail and when they came to the fork in the road they unpacked the money into the wagons.

"Wolf look at this," Thomas instructed.

On the side of the wagon were large claw marks. The cover of the wagon was ripped to shreds and the meat was gone.

"Cat. A very large cat, Puma. We don't have time for this. Load up the money and hitch the horses up. We must go, Bach."

When they got done unloading the money, they came out from behind the bush. Standing in front of them were Siksika braves. No horses, on foot, with weapons drawn.

One large brave came and stepped in front of Red Fox and spoke to him. Wolf starting talking to him and he drew his attention to him.

"What are they saying, Wolf?" Thomas asked.

"They want to know what we are doing on Siksika land. They want to know why we have a white man at our side. They will take us back to their village. Forget what we have gotten Bach. Just go with them. They will not let us go without answers to their questions. Lay your gun on the ground and walk away from it," Wolf instructed.

Wolf talked again to the Siksika brave. "We must ride our horses to their village and meet with their chief. Just do as they say. No quick moves or it will be your last. They will kill you first. Their hate for the white man it greater than that of the Crow," Wolf ended.

The men climbed onto their horses and the braves walked along side holding the reins. Once over the hill the Siksika mounted their horses and the braves took them over the ridge down a path. Halfway down the mountain Wolf heard a bird call. He acted like it was nothing. But he knew that it was Puma. "Help was on the way." He thought. They rode into the village. There seemed to be a lot of women and children but not too many braves. Thomas tried counting them but could only count 23. They dismounted and the Siksika place all three men into a hut.

"Bach did you hear that bird on the trail? It was Puma. He will bring help," Wolf said.

"I didn't hear anything. I was too busy thinking about Nancy and how I might never see her again," Thomas ended.

Just then a brave entered the hut. He talked to Wolf and left.

"He wants to know if you are a Friend. If the white people called, 'Friends' are your brother or Father? I told him no and that we were just wanting to visit them. It is better not to lie to them. They can tell a lie. I also told them that we need food and water," Wolf ended.

"Where are all the men? I only counted around 20 or so, the rest is just children and women." Thomas stated.

"The white man and the Siksika have been fighting for years. Their men have died in battle. The white man has not come past the Arrow Rock. They will not pass that mountain. If we show no signs of fight, they might let us go. But I'm not to sure about you Thomas Bach. They might kill you just because you are white," Wolf ended.

Then two children entered the hut with a brave. They were carrying food and water. Thomas noticed that one of the children was white.

"Wolf, he's a white child. Maybe he's Nancy's son, Kyle?" Thomas questioned.

Wolf talked to the brave and when Thomas heard the name Kyle, the white child looked up.

"I know Kyle," the boy said. "He is fishing with the others.

Do you know him or his family? Do you bring news from our town? Is help on the way?"

"How many children from the town are here?" Thomas asked

"There are four of us. I'm John. Me and Kyle are the only ones from Chester; the other two are from Helena. I'll tell Kyle that you are looking for him. That you bring news about his family, you do have news about our parents don't you?" John said with a questioning look on his face

"It has been so long since I have seen my family."

The brave then pushed the children out the door.

"Wolf did you hear? We have found Kyle. Maybe this will work out. Just maybe we all can be together again," Thomas said.

"Or maybe we will all die together," Red Fox spoke up.

"We must try to escape. We must free ourselves before it is to late."

"NO! We must wait this out. See what the Siksika will do with us," Wolf said.

"Yes... I forget that we MUST wait. We must sit here and WAIT... we must protect this white man that has sent us to our graves. I will wait... but not to long. If I see my chance I will run. I will fight. What say you brother? Will you just wait to die? Will you die for this white man? Or will you fight and die with honor?" Red Fox spoke with passion.

"Red Fox your words speak of a young brave. You will learn that sometimes it is better to wait, than act foolish." Wolf ended.

Thomas sat quietly as he ate. It was a mix of red meats and fish, a few roots and a broth. It wasn't that bad he thought.

"This really isn't that bad tasting. Other than the stale bread I could eat this everyday" Thomas said.

There was a still silence in the wigwam. Then someone opened the flap. The men stood up and greeted two braves and an older gentleman. They sat facing each other.

"I will speak so the white man can understand. I am Kotoka, the oldest living Siksika Indian. Our chief was killed over a year ago by the white man's army. We have no chief, but since I am the oldest, I will speak for my people. My questions to you are why are you have come and why were you at the Friends home?" Kotoka queried.

"Well they are friends of mine and I came to visit them. I had hired these two to take me to see them. But when I got there they were dead" Thomas said.

"Yes, I was very angry when I learned of their deaths," Kotoka said.

"Then why did you kill them?" Thomas asked.

"We did not kill them. Men came looking for them, white men. One carried a star on his chest. They shot them, then they laid our arrows beside the bodies. We drove the killers out of our lands. We have not seen them in well over a year. The missionaries were our friends. They taught us about following one great sprit. They taught me the words of the white man." Kotoka said.

"McKenzie" Thomas breathed.

"Who is this McKenzie?" Kotoka demanded.

"Sheriff McKenzie. The man with the star on his chest. He is dead. These great Crow braves killed him and his men just about a week ago. He was an evil man." Thomas said.

"Tell me your names Crow braves." Kotoka demanded.

"I am Wolf, son of the Crow Chief Perits-Sinkpas. This is my brother Red Fox. We must return to our father as soon as we can. Tell me Kotoka, is this all that is left of your village?" Wolf questioned.

"Yes, many of our people have been captured by the white man and taken from here. We are slowly fading into the earth. Our time on this land is coming to a close," Kotoka sadly stated.

Just then the men heard a noise outside. A young brave came into the wigwam and spoke into Kotoka's ear.

"Everyone outside," Kotoka said.

The men all stood outside looking up to the ridge. The men could see about fifty braves on horse back. In the front was Medicine Crow.

"Father," Wolf explained.

Sitting beside him was Puma. Wolf held up his hand and yelled to his father. Slowly the Crow rode down the road into the village.

"He comes in peace. He wants to speak with you Kotoka," Wolf said.

The Crow came to a stop in front of the men. They dismounted and stood face to face with Kotoka.

"I'm Perits-Sinkpas Chief of the Crow. I have come to take back my sons and Mr. Bach. They shall be prisoners no more." Medicine Crow intoned.

"Prisoners? Why they are not prisoners. We were just eating. Will you please eat with us Chief? We can talk," Kotoka invited.

"Father, you came swiftly. You must have ridden day and night," Red Fox said.

"No, we left before we knew what was going on. We met Puma

on the trail. We bring news that we must talk about." Medicine Crown said.

"Is Nancy all right? Tell me that is okay.' Thomas asked.

"Yes, she is fine, but now I must speak to everyone." Everyone then entered the Wigwam.

"We are being followed by the white man army. They have many men. They will be here by morning's light. We must prepare for battle. The Crow will run no more. We will make a stand," The Chief stated imperially.

"This army, they are coming for you and also my people. We are the keepers of the mountains. Once we are gone the white man will destroy this land with home and cattle. Our way of life will be gone. We are not many, but we will fight with you Chief. Let our blood spill together onto this land." Kotoka agreed.

The Chief and Kotoka looked at each other and knodded. The flap opened once again and food and water was brought in. Thomas noticed another white boy was serving the food. Thomas stood up and left the wigwam. He waited outside, when the flap opened again and the boy stepped out.

"Kyle? Is your name Kyle? I bring news of your mother," Thomas said.

"My name is Kyle."

"Did you live in Chester and is your mother's name Nancy?" Thomas asked.

"Yes! Yes, is she alive?" Kyle asked.

"She is alive and well!"

"And my father?"

"I'm afraid your father died, but your mother misses you so much," Thomas answered.

"How do you know my mother?" Kyle questioned.

"Well, we got to be friends in Helena. Your mother made it to Helena. Then she worked for Mrs. Cater, a horse rancher. I met Nancy when I bought my horses and wagon. Your mother and I are very close Kyle. Your mother is waiting for us back at Chester. She is in the same old house. I will take you back as soon as possible. Are you okay with all this?" Thomas asked.

Kyle just looked at the ground and then he spoke up. "You said you are really good friends with my mother. How good of friend?" Kyle questioned.

"Well I want to be honest with you Kyle. I want to tell you the truth. Your mother and I are in love. We were married a few weeks ago by the Crow Chief." Thomas explained.

"I don't believe you! Mother would never marry anyone after my father." Kyle exclaimed.

"Listen, we didn't plan on this, it just happened. We found each other and the most important thing is that we love each other. We both want you to come back home. I don't want to take the place of your father. No one could do that, but don't you want your mother to be happy?" Thomas asked.

"Well yes, but that was my fathers home, He built it with his own hands." Kyle turned his back to Thomas. "I remember him as a strong man. I don't ever want to forget him. I wish he was also waiting for me back home." Kyle said.

"Kyle, you will always have those memories. You will always have that feeling. I just hope that we can be friends. Okay, Kyle just friends, Thomas smiled.

Kyle turned and ran into Thomas's arms crying. "Yes, I guess but it wouldn't be the same without him. I just want to go back home and sleep in my room and see my mother." Kyle cried.

"We are all hopeful that we can start building the town back up again. We want to get people to come back and start over. Just think, you can be there for that. A new beginning, a new start" Thomas explained.

Thomas and Kyle talked until they noticed the sun starting to set. "Kyle, you need to go and get your stuff together and come back here so we can leave. I must talk to Kotoka about you and the other children," Thomas said.

Thomas reentered the wigwam. Medicine Crow and Kotoka turned and looked at him.

"Chief! I have found Kyle. I have talked to him and I want to take him home. Is it oaky with Kotoka?" Thomas ended.

"Kotoka and I have been talking also. We have this plan tell him, Kotoka, what we have come up with," Medicine Crow said.

"Our two tribes will join as one. We will lead this one tribe to fight against the white mans army. We will lead them to the open field at the bottom of the mountain. Medicine Crow will line up at the end of the field and will charge the army. Our men will come from the edges of the woods, firing arrows from the sides. This will be our fight, we will win. We will fight for our fathers, for the horror of our lost braves. We would like for you to take all the white children in your wagons and start back to your town. I have sent Wolf and Puma to get the wagons. They should be back soon. When they arrive we will split the money three ways." Kotoka ended.

"Yes Kotoka knows about the money. This way everyone is happy, except the white man's army. By tomorrow's setting sun the army will be gone. We will climb higher into the mountains and live out our lives. Do you understand, Thomas Bach?" Medicine Crown asked.

"Yes. I fully agree. It is the only way," Thomas said.

Just then the flap opened and Wolf and Puma entered.

"We have gotten the wagons and horses. They are ready for travel. Thomas you need to round up the children to go." Wolf said as he had thrown the money bags to the floor.

Thomas agreed with Wolf, "While you and Kotoka count out the money. I will gather up the children for our journey. I need not be here while you do that. I trust you chief. I really would like my share to be placed into the main wagon with the big set of horses," Thomas said.

"You trust us Bach?" Kotoka questioned.

"Yes, because I really have what I really want. The money will just help settle some debts," Thomas said.

Kotoka stood up and walked to Thomas and placed his hands on Thomas's shoulders.

"You will always be welcome in our village. There are few white men that I trust. You will be the last one, Thomas Bach." Then Kotoka takes off his necklace and places it on Thomas.

"Carry this when you come and up on the mountain. A safe travel to you" Kotoka instructed.

Thomas hugged Kotoka and Medicine Crow. "And you also have a safe travel and a long life. You are a great people. Return to the land and may you always have an early spring," Thomas said smiling.

"Come, Bach, let's get the children and load up the wagons," Red Fox ordered.

Thomas, Wolf and Red Fox loaded up the children. As they got the one into the wagon, Medicine Crow threw a large bag into Thomas' wagon.

"This is your share, Thomas Bach. We gave you most of the paper money and some gold coin. You must leave now. We must prepare for our battle in the morning."

"You heard him children. Does anyone know how to drive a wagon?" One boy raised his hand. "Good, you can drive the other wagon. Just follow me. We will go to the top of the road, turn left and proceed to Arrow Rock and camp for the night. Then in the morning we will start our three day journey to Chester." Thomas ended. The children yelled and jumped up and down.

The wagons slowly climbed the hill. Thomas turned for one last look at the village. The sun was almost set, but the moon shone down upon Kotoka and Medicine Crow. Thomas thought to himself. "This maybe the last time I will see them. At least they will die together."

Thomas turned around and guided the wagon along the trail, using the moon to lead him. He looked up at.

"Ah, Nancy's moon will guide us. Don't worry Nancy. I'm coming home."

Chapter Eight
The Waiting Game

Nancy awoke with the sun shining though her bedroom window. Laying next to her was Laura. She was sleeping soundly and sucking her thumb.

"Laura. Laura are you awake?" Nancy asked.

"What? Yes, I'm awake," She said rubbing her eyes.

Nancy then heard a knock on the door.

"Yes. What is it?" Nancy asked.

We are all awake Mrs. Bach. We will go downstairs and start some breakfast. "David said though the door. "We have a surprise for breakfast."

"That's fine. Me and Laura will get dressed and be down in a minute."

Nancy made the bed and her Laura and she dressed. She went into the other rooms and noticed how tidy and neat everything was. The beds were made and the curtains drawn back to let in the light. The two climbed down the stairs and Nancy smelled something coming from the kitchen.

"What is that smell? I know what it smells like. . .but it couldn't be," Nancy told Laura.

"Mary, Janet are those eggs that I smell cooking?"

"Yes, they are. The army dropped off these early this morning along with this meat," Mary said.

"That's wonderful! What kind of meat is it?' Nancy asked.

"I'm not sure. It is wrapped in a burlap sack and it looks like a leg. Me and David cut some meat off. It's in the frying pan," Janet said.

Nancy looked at the meat. It was ham. "It is ham. How many hams are there?"

David spoke up, "The army gave us five. The wagons from Helena are starting to arrive. They also brought something else; you need to look outside in the back yard and there's this note from Cornel Mitchell."

Nancy crossed to the back door. She looked out the window. She walked out onto the porch, like she was walking in a trance. What she saw made her unsteady. She had to hold herself up against the porch rail. There standing in her yard were two freshened milk cows, a mule, laying chickens running everywhere.

"Let me see that note, David," she grabbed it from him and read it.

"*Dear Mrs. Bach:*

I had my men pick up some extra things while they were in town. There will also be grain in the barn awaiting you. The cows are freshened, so the children will have milk. The chickens will lay eggs and the mule you will need next spring for your planting. In another day or so, there will be more supplies coming to you to help out with rebuilding this town. Now my mind can rest knowing that the children will have enough to eat and drink.

The rest is up to you Mrs. Bach. You must get this town into shape, because upon my victorious return, everything needs to be in order.

Warmest Regards,

Colonel Robert C. Mitchell"

"What does the note say?" Taylor asked.

"It says let's round up these animals and get them into the barn," Nancy said, "Mary finish the breakfast. We don't want to waste it."

Nancy and the other children started to round up the animals. The cows and the mule were no problem, but the chicken's ran everywhere. The children chased after each of them.

"If you can get a few into the barn, the rest will follow," David said.

They placed the animals in the barn and closed the doors.

"Breakfast is ready!" Yelled Mary. "Wash up everyone."

Everyone ran to the table. Mary and Janet had made a feast fit for kings. Scrambled eggs, potatoes and ham. Were placed on the table.

Nancy said, "Let us pray. Oh heavenly Father we wish to thank you for this wonderful bounty of food. We also would like to thank you for the animals and thank Colonel Mitchell for his kind heart. Let these children learn from your gifts and may it help them grow. In Jesus name. Amen."

The group ate their breakfast; nothing was wasted. Nancy sat back on her chair, "Janet, what have you done with the rest of the meat that you unwrapped?"

"I cut the whole ham up and I will get it ready be canned. I found some jars and lids under the sink," Janet explained.

"Now listen, while Janet is canning ham, David, you and Taylor go to the barn and settle the animals. I want the cows in the big stalls and the mule can be turned outside in the back fenced area. You may need to fix the fence before letting him out. I think there is some dry wood laying around the barn. Then, I want you two to build some nesting boxes for the chickens. Mary, Laura and I will go to the old school house and start cleaning up. Does everyone know what their jobs are?" Nancy asked.

"Yes, Mrs. Bach," The children said.

Laura and Nancy walked to the old school house. From the outside it looked to be in good shape. It wasn't until Nancy opened the front door that she saw the mess.

"My goodness, Laura! We have our work cut out for us today," Nancy said.

The desks and chairs were all broken and stacked in a large pile. Nancy tried to pull the pile apart, but it wouldn't move.

"Laura I really don't know how we are going to do this?"

"Well, Mrs. Bach, maybe we can help? Private Johnson at your service. Colonel Mitchell left instructions that we were to help. According to the Colonel, we have nothing else to do; so we are to help you get this town into shipshape. Just tell me what you want my men and me to do and its done," Private Johnson ended.

"Let's see. How many men do you have left?"

"Fifteen."

"Well then, since it is a beautiful day out, I want you and your men to take all of the furniture that is either broken or useless and cut it up into small sticks for the cooking stove. Anything that we don't need we'll use for fires and then we will see what we have left," Nancy ended.

"You heard her men. Let's move! Start with three men per house. Everything that is useless place in the street. We will deal with it later." Johnson ordered.

Nancy and Laura watched the men work. Within a few hours, the town's main street had a large stack of damaged odds and ends. The desks from the school were of no use and couldn't be fixed.

"Private Johnson, I'll need tables and chairs from the houses to use in the school. Also school books, lots of books. There has got to be some school books around here somewhere. What was her name? The old school teacher…Mrs. Shaffer. She lived down the street, last house on the left. There might be some school books in her place." Nancy ended.

The men worked until the sun was over head. The main street was almost cleaned up and thing s were starting to look up.

"Lunch!" yelled Johnson.

Nancy and Laura walked back to the house and entered the

kitchen. Janet had fresh bread cut up for ham sandwiches.

"Looks like ham again, Mrs. Bach," Janet said.

"Oh that's fine. The bread looks great." Nancy said as she stood at the back door.

"Boys lunch is ready!"

The boys came running with Taylor carrying a small pail.

"And what is in the pail that you are holding Taylor?" Nancy questioned.

"Milk, Mrs. Bach. David and I milked the cow," Taylor said smiling.

"She didn't give very much milk, but I figured if we grain her up over the next few days she'll start to give more," David said.

Nancy poured the milk into cups and filled them half way up. "A half cup is better than no cup."

Mary sat two pies down on the table.

"One is blueberry and the other one is blackberry. Janet and I are going picking again this afternoon, if it is okay Mrs. Bach. We want to can some for the winter," Mary explained.

"That would be great. You know I think, I am going to save my milk for my pie. Just pour it on top," Nancy said.

After lunch Nancy began. "Now that we are done eating lets hear how everything is going. David and Taylor, how's the barn coming?"

"The cows are penned in, watered and fed. The mule is outside also," David said.

"The chickens are all in the barn and we are working on the boxes." Taylor added.

"Girls, your plans are to pick berries today?" Nancy asked.

"Yes, Mrs. Bach. After we clean up the dishes," Janet said.

"Oh, don't worry about that. Let Laura and I take care of those. You girls run along and pick," Nancy said.

"Can I go with Janet and Mary to pick?" Laura asked

"Well, if you want to, dear. You be good and you two keep an eye on her," Nancy said.

"Yes, Mrs. Bach," The girls answered.

After Nancy had cleaned up the kitchen she sat down at the table. She stared out the window and wondered about Thomas. Now with the children all out working, she has some time to reflect. It had been over fifteen days since Thomas had left. She wondered if she would ever see him again. As Nancy held her necklace, she had a deep feeling that Thomas was still alive. It was just the waiting that was so hard. At least the children kept her mind off of Thomas," She thought.

There was a sturdy knock on the door.

Nancy jumped in her seat, as she heard the rapping on the door. "Yes?"

"Mrs. Bach, we have everything in place," Private Johnson said. "We moved all the junk to the backside of town. Tables and chairs are in the school house and we found over twenty school books."

"That's great. Good job, Johnson!" Nancy said.

"Also, another wagon form Helena came and we have more supplies for you."

"What more do you have?"

"Well, buckets, rakes, brooms and paint and brushes."

"What colors? If you have any white, just plain white please paint the school and the church after your men fix the windows. Also I have been thinking, it's never too early to start cutting firewood for the winter. six or seven cords will be nice." Nancy said smiling, "for me and the children."

"The Colonel said we were to do everything within reason that you asked. That sounds within reason. Yes, we will get right on it," Johnson said.

Nancy watched as Johnson cross the street and talked to the other soldiers. They said not a word but went straight to work. Suddenly Nancy felt a little sick and light headed. Her stomach didn't feel right. She sat back down and drank some cool water. "I hope I'm not coming down with anything," she thought. She felt like that for a few minutes then just as fast as it had come on she felt fine.

Over the next few days, the town started to take shape and the school with it's new paint job looked like new. The church shone bright in the sun and firewood was everywhere. Nancy had asked to six-seven cords but the men had cut over ten. The animals started to feel at home and they gave plenty of milk. The army even delivered two beef cattle for winter slaughter. They would be in good shape for winter to hang in the meat house. Nancy was also having more sick spells. They seemed to hit her up to three times a day. She didn't want to alarm the children but she worried that she had caught something and the children would get it next.

On the eighteenth day that Thomas had been gone, Private Johnson appeared at the kitchen door again.

"Mrs. Bach, I was following the Colonel's orders and sent scouts out on the twelfth day. We seem to have a problem," Johnson said.

"What is the problem?" Nancy asked.

"Our riders found horses. Soldiers' horses that were running free with out riders. One of them was the Colonel's."

"Oh, my God!" Nancy exclaimed as she slid down onto a chair.

"We think that the whole regiment was wiped out. The men have started to desert. Last night, I had four men leave in the middle of the night. I don't know how long I can hold these men here," Johnson ended.

"Were there any large work horses found with the others?" Nancy questioned.

"No, ma'am, just army issue. There was no sign of life, other than the horses."

"Tell me, Johnson, what were your orders if the Colonel didn't return?" Nancy questioned.

"We were to stay here until further orders. If no further instructions came after six months we were to report to the nearest fort, which would be on the other side of Helena. But with the way the men leaving, by the end of the week, I'll be down to just a few, maybe six men," Johnson said

"Then you shall follow orders, but tell me, Johnson, do you still have a doctor here?" she asked.

"Yes, Doc. Miller. Why are the children all right?"

"Yes, they are fine, but I would like for everyone to have a checkup before the winter hits and there's no doctor. Plus, I have been feeling a little sick lately."

"Sure, I'll send him over. He'll be here in a few minutes," with that Johnson left to gather up the doctor.

Nancy got the children together.

Listen, I have asked the Army doctor to come and pay us a visit, so we can get checked out. I'm even getting a look over. I just want him to check everyone out before winter hits," Nancy ended.

"Is it gonna hurt? No shots, right?" Janet questioned.

"Well, I don't think so."

There was a knock at the door.

"Mrs. Bach? I'm Doctor Miller."

"Yes, I was wondering if you could give the children and me a look over. Just to make sure we are in good shape," Nancy asks.

"Sure, I'm not doing anything else. Not much wounded while we are staying here. Who first?" Doc Miller asked.

Everyone just stood there. No one moved or volunteered.

"All right, I'll go first. Children just wait here around the table. I shouldn't be very long," Nancy left with the Doctor and went upstairs. Once in the room, Nancy turned to the doctor and spoke up.

"Listen, Doc I want you to examine me, but the children need it too. I haven't been feeling very well lately and I don't want the children to worry," Nancy ended.

"Well why don't you tell me what has been wrong with you and let's take a look at you shall we," Doc Miller said.

After about 10 minutes with the doctor, Nancy came walking down the stairs with a wide-eyed look on her face.

"Who's next? See that wasn't too bad."

"What did he say? Are you okay? Did he give you a shot?" The children were all trying to speak at once.

"Well," Nancy pause, "Well, children it looks like I'm pregnant." Nancy said as she sat down at the table.

"That's it! I'm not going upstairs," Taylor said.

"Why?" Nancy asked.

"I don't want to be pregnant," Taylor said.

"Taylor, that means she is gonna have a baby. She's not sick," David explained. "You can't get pregnant."

All the children burst out in laughing. They hugged Nancy and one by one they went upstairs for their checkups. When everyone was done, the doctor met with them all at the table.

"Well, it looks like everyone is in fine shape. You children need to take up the slack and I don't want Mrs. Bach lifting and tugging anything heavy. When your husband comes home, tell him he'll need to fix up a nursery." Doc Miller said as he left.

Nancy sat at the table with her eyes still wide. She had a look of disbelief on her face. She thought back, "On the trail, that night in the wagon. It would have to be, then again when we were married. Pregnant. I'm pregnant and without Thomas. Boy, will he be surprised when he gets home; if he makes it home."

"Mrs. Bach? Are you all right Mrs. Bach?" Janet asked worriedly.

"Yes, I'm fine. It's just gonna take a little time to sink in," Nancy said.

"When will your husband be home, Mrs. Bach? I bet you can't wait to tell him the good news?" David said.

"Yes, the good news. I'll also bet he'll be surprised when he get home. First it was you fine children, then the arrival of the animals and food. Now this. Why yes he will be surprised. I can't wait to see the look on his face. Children, we must still work. We must get this town into shape," Nancy ended.

Over the next two days, Nancy and the children worked hard on the town, painting and fixing fences. By the end of the week Nancy noticed that the army was down to just a few men. She walked over to Private Johnson.

"Mr. Johnson, how many men do you now have left?" Nancy asked.

"Well, Mrs. Bach, only five of us. The rest took the wagons, most of the guns and just left us with a few horses and enough ammo for awhile. I was thinking this morning and I wanted to come and talk to you. If no one wants that old blacksmith house, do you think that if would be okay if I live in it? My father taught me blacksmithing, before I went into the army," Johnson asked.

"Why I think that would be a good idea. You could live and work there. Start from scratch. But what about the Army?" Nancy asked.

"Thank you Mrs. Bach and about the army, what army? All the men are either dead or gone. I wouldn't last by myself trying to get to the other fort. So I guess I'm just going to be a regular guy. The town's blacksmith. I will not say anything to the others and by morning they will all be gone anyway," Johnson said.

Nancy went the barn. "David? David, are you in here?" What she saw stopped her in her tracks. It was David and Janet sitting on an old hay bale kissing and holding hands. They both stood up when Nancy walked in.

"Well what do we have here?" A long dead silence was then broken by Nancy, "Well David, Janet do you want to explain this?" Janet demanded.

"Its my fault, Mrs. Bach. I wanted Janet to follow me into the barn. I'm the one that kissed her, she had nothing to do with it, only the good part," David said smiling.

"How long has this been going on young man?" Nancy asked sternly.

For about a month," Janet blurted out, "We love each other and in a year we want to get married!"

"Well, while we are sharing the same house, I'll have to trust you. I'm not saying you can't see one and another but what I'm saying is that you two need a little supervision. Do I have an understanding with you two?" Nancy said.

"Yes, Mrs. Bach," David and Janet said.

"Now, Janet please go round up the children for supper. The fire should be fine. And David, we need to talk. You said when you first came here that your father owned the granary and mill?"

"Yes, ma'am. I helped to run it. We never quite got the water wheel working right, but it was my family business." David answered.

"You said that you thought that you and Janet are going to get married next year. I think that you will need a home after you get married. I also think that you need to start working on your family's house and mill. I think you need to be a working man. A man with his own business. What do you think?" Nancy asked.

"But who will take care of Taylor?" David asked.

"He will be fine. He can go to you house at night and can come over here during the day. This will free you up so you can work getting things fixed up. How about it David? Are you up to it? Are you ready to become a man, take responsibility and start your life start again?" Nancy ended.

David said smiling. "Yes Mrs. Bach. I sure am. Can I tell Janet what going on?"

"Of course you can. You can sleep tonight at my house but in the morning you'll need to start getting things together at your new home," Nancy ended.

David jumped up and ran out of the barn. Nancy thought to herself, "How many house's are there? Giving each child his or her there old home when they are ready, will help this town to grow. Tomorrow, two new homes and two new businesses will start. Things are looking up."

That night after tucking the children in bed, Nancy stayed up sewing the children's clothes. In the morning she would start with the schooling. They would need to have new clothes that fit. Laura was all snuggled down into Nancy's bed sleeping soundly. She was only supposed to spend one night in Nancy's bed, but she needed to sleep with someone. For now she could sleep with her until Thomas came home.

Nancy didn't sleep well that night. In her dreams she could see Thomas fighting off someone and then he lay dead on that mountain.

That damn mountain! That damn money! The dream was so real she got up by herself and did all the chores. She was frying breakfast when the first of the family came into the kitchen.

"David, you're up early, aren't you?" Nancy asked.

"Yes, I wanted to get an early start. I'll do the milking, and then gather the eggs. Feed and then I'll be in for breakfast," David said.

"All done," Nancy said.

"What?"

"It's all done. I felt like doing everything this morning. Breakfast will be ready in a few minutes. Why don't you go and wake up everyone," Nancy said.

"You know what the doctor said, Mrs. Bach. A woman in your condition shouldn't be doing barn work," David stated.

"David, don't worry about my condition. I'm a big girl. I think I can take care of myself but thanks for worrying about me. Now go and get the others," Nancy said.

As the children all sat around the table, they heard a knock at the door.

"Who is it?" Mary asked.

"It's me, Mr. Johnson. Is Mrs. Bach home?"

Nancy opened the door and Mr. Johnson was standing there holding his hat in his hand.

"Private Johnson."

"Oh, Mrs. Bach. Everyone else left last night and then this morning the last wagon showed up. After I told them they were free to go they got all their things and left everything else. So, I thought that you and the children could use some of this stuff. I took what I needed all ready. And it's Mr. Johnson now; I'm no private anymore," Johnson ended.

"Children lets go and see what we can use. Come hurry, it's looking like rain," Nancy said.

Nancy went over to the wagons. They were full of food and supplies. One wagon had dried beef and feed for the animals. The other had kitchen supplies, like pots and pans. Nancy looked under one cover and discovered little bags of seeds. There were flower, tomato, corn, wheat and some gourds she had never heard of.

"Hey, kids it's looking like we are going to have a large garden next year. Unload these things into the house Janet. David take the feed into the barn," Nancy walked over to the house and turned to look at that storm the was approaching over the mountain.

"Hurry up children! A storm is brewing. I don't want the supplies to get wet," Nancy ordered.

Nancy started feeling sick again. She just wanted to lay down. She climbed the stairs and looked out the hallway window. "This storm looks bad," she thought. "I sure hope it passes soon." Rain starting hitting the window pane as Nancy went to lie down. The next few days seemed to linger on. David worked in the granary. Mr. Johnson worked on his blacksmith shop. Nancy everyday after lunch took the children to the school house and taught them lessons for a few hours. Even David joined the group in the afternoons.

With every day that passed Nancy's hopes for Thomas's safe return grew slim. The Colonel's horse returning without him, made Nancy uneasy. Laura still slept with her and Nancy cried herself to sleep almost every night. She would lay awake longing and waiting for Thomas to return. She still felt deep inside that Thomas was alive. She just could figure not out why he hadn't return to her.

Chapter Nine
The Journey Home

As Thomas meandered his wagon over the trail, the moonlight light guided his way. Kyle sat by his side and they made small talk. As the wagon turned the hill, the moon shone brightly upon the arrow rock.

"Look," Kyle pointed, "The moon is hitting that rock. It looks like it is glowing. Is that where we are camping tonight?" Kyle asked.

"Yes, Kyle. There is a lot of history behind that rock. One day I'll tell you the story of all of this. It make's for an interesting tale," Thomas said.

The wagon came to a stop along side the rock. "Let's unhitch the horses and get them some water for the night. I also want everyone to report to me afterward, so I can get some bearings on who is who?" Thomas said.

Thomas started a fire and watched the boys take care of the horses. The boys came back with wood for the fire. Thomas counted six boys, including Kyle.

"Now line up and give me your names, where you last lived and ages, if you know them," Thomas ordered.

The first boy stepped up. “Garrett Wilson, seventeen. Chester, Montana. My parents owned the bank. I was taken in the raid by the Crow. My father and mother were both killed. I really have nothing to go home too, but I would like to see the others find homes.” Garrett said.

“Brian Shue, fourteen, from the East, Pennsylvania, I think. I was taken by the Siksika a few years back. I have no idea where my parents are. We were coming to Helena to live with my aunt and uncle.”

“Terry Friend. twelve. I came here with my dad and mom. They were the missionaries that were killed last year. I also have nowhere to go.”

“Nathan Custer. eleven. My family owned the saloon in Chester. They weren’t killed right away. The crow Chief kept then alive for a week or two. Then one day, my father tried to kill him. One of his sons killed my father and then went up the steps and killed my mother. I don’t remember why my dad tried to kill the chief. I was there but I can’t place what happened.”

“Tucker Workman. eleven. I don’t remember much. I am also from Chester, but the Siksika took me two years before the others. I was fishing and they just took me. Really I don’t remember much, But I’m pretty sure I’m eleven, at least that’s what I’ve been told.”

“Now, I think that everyone knows Kyle. Let’s bed down for the night boys. I think I’m sleeping outside tonight. How about you fellas? Want to breath the fresh air tonight?” Thomas asked.

“Sounds good to us, Mr. Bach,” the boys said.

The group gathered around the fire and laid down on the ground. They slept until dawn broke through the trees. Thomas gathered the food and started to make breakfast.

“Boys, get up and gather some wood. Garrett, go over the hill and get some water for breakfast and the horses. Boys, let’s get ready for breakfast so we can start home.” Thomas ended.

The fire was going well and Thomas placed the cook pot over the it. Garrett came running up to the camp.

"Mr. Bach, Mr. Bach. The Army. The Army is coming. We must hide," Garrett yelled as he ran into the wagon.

The boys started to run around. "Boys, why are you hiding? The Army will not hurt you. They are looking for Indians, not white children. Now get over here." The boys gathered around the fire. They could hear horses riding hard up the trail.

"Hold it right there! No one move!"

"No one is moving and put that damn gun down. It's just me and the boys. No one else," Thomas stated.

"Are you sure your not hiding any Crow?"

"No, and you are?" Thomas questioned.

"Colonel Mitchell, U.S. Army, and you, sir?" Mitchell demanded.

"Thomas Bach. We are headed for Chester."

"Thomas Bach, Nancy's husband?"

"Yes. How do you know her? How is Nancy?" Thomas asked.

Thomas looked behind the Colonel to see a line of soldiers on horses. "Nancy is fine. We were at Chester a little over a week ago. Now about those boys?

Surely they are not all your sons?" The Colonel said.

"No, they were taken by the Siksika. I came and took them back to Chester. To start over," Thomas said.

"So, you just walked into Blackfoot country and took back boys that they stole from God knows where? You don't look like a gun slinger." Mitchell stated.

"No, I traded for them. Guns aren't always the way. Sometimes it works better if you just sit down and talk like civil men," Thomas ended.

"You two there. Step up front here, state your names," the Colonel ordered.

"Garrett."

"Brian."

"You two look a little red to me." The men started to laugh. "Do you have a little Indian in you? Or are you so dirty you just look like it? Are you in need of a bath?" The colonel said, laughing along with his men.

"Well, all these boys are in need of a bath and what they really need to get back home," Thomas said.

"Let me ask you this and you had better give me a straight answer!" the Colonel raised his gun to the boys. "Have you seen the Crow or the Siksika in the last day or two?' Mitchell asked.

Thomas answered after a long pause. "Yes, I have, I saw the Crow after I made my deal with the Siksika chief. I think they said they were going further into the mountains. Away from the white man," Thomas said.

"So, they are trying to live on this God forsaken mountain?" the Colonel asked.

"I do believe the name is Elkhorn Mountain, Colonel."

The Colonel just looked at Thomas. "Dickerson, get over here! Look in the wagons for anyone else. Let's go men. We have the savages on the run. Good day to you, Mr. Bach. Good luck getting your children home to Chester," the Colonel said as he rode off.

Dickerson looked into the wagons and left. Thomas stared at the men as they rode over the hill. "Maybe I should have warned him of his impending doom. Maybe I should have told him what was waiting for him in the field," Thomas thought. "But I think I'll just let it play out. I can't choose a side when it comes to this."

Thomas and the boys ate quickly and hitched up the horses. Then off they went. Thomas took the lead, climbing the side of the mountain range. To the right he could look down and see for miles. Thomas could see an open valley and field about four miles long. They stopped for a brief respite.

"Lunch!" Thomas yelled. "Everyone water the horses and eat only three flat meats each. It's got to last another day and a half." Thomas said.

As Thomas and the boys stretched their legs, they could hear a bugle blow in the distant valley. Thomas took out his scope and that is when he could see them. He spotted the Crow chief and a few braves in the meadow. They were being chased by the Army. The boys gathered beside of Thomas and watched. Thomas watched with excitement as the Crow led the Army right into the trap. The Chief stopped at the edge of the woodline, turned his braves around and charged. Thomas could see arrows, being fired from the woods, hitting the army. Men and horses fell to the ground. The Army tried to retreat but the Siksika closed in from the rear. The army was being fired on by all four sides. Thomas saw the Colonel fall from his horse and land hard on the ground. One by one, each soldier was killed. Only a few Indians were killed in the attack. Almost as soon as it started, it was over. The Crow turned each soldier over and stabbed them in the chest. They took whatever they could use and then the Crow and Siksika all grouped up. They were just going to leave the Army to rot in the afternoon sun. As the Indians started to make their retreat into the mountains, Thomas nearly jumped out of his boots when Garrett picked up his horn and blew a few loud blows. Thomas looked through his scope at the Crow chief. He saw him raise his spear. He was saying goodbye. As Thomas looked over the dead bodies, he saw Wolf and Puma carrying someone into the woods. As he looked closer, Thomas could tell it was Red Fox. His chest was open and he was not moving. Thomas gasped as he realized that Red Fox was dead. He closed his scope and turned and faced the boys.

"It's over. The Army is no more. They will send more troops. They will not find the Crow or Siksika. They will talk and dance about this day. They will tell this story to their children. This is a great day for the last of the American Indians. Let's get going," Thomas ended.

As Thomas climbed into the wagon, he sat down and thought to himself, "Maybe I should have told the Army about what the Indians had planned, but instead I let it play itself out. This will haunt me the rest of my life." Slapping the reins, "Let's head home boys!" he said.

The sun beat down on the wagons as they moved down the mountain. In the distance, Thomas saw a storm coming. The clouds were dark and heavy. He could see the rain pouring down like thick fog in the horizon.

"Boys, let's find someplace to bed down for the night."

"But we still have hours of daylight left," Terry said.

"Yes, but look to the north. Those clouds look bad. It's better to get set up before the storm hits. Pull the wagons into those trees. These big oaks will shield us and the horses. It looks like it's going to be a bad one," Thomas said.

They placed the wagons side to side and left about 15 feet between the wagons. Thomas took a canvas tarp and stretched it over both the wagons and made a dry area. He took rope and tied down both wagons.

"Mr. Bach, don't you think this is a little bit much?" Brian asked.

"Brian, I was in a storm one time and we lost everything. We are just taking precautions. Now boys, gather firewood and put it under the tar to stay dry," Thomas ordered.

It was about this time that Thomas felt a cold chill go down his spine. The bear claw markings started to burn. "It's just the storm," Thomas thought.

The wind started up, and a light rain started falling. "Boys, into this wagon. Tie back the canvas and sit in the middle." Thomas yelled as the wind started to blow harder.

A loud clap of thunder hit the mountain; it was almost deafening. Thomas and the boys could feel the wagon rock back and forth. Thomas could hear the rain hitting the wagon cover. He could also hear the horses pacing back and forth.

"Listen, one of us is going to have to go outside with the horses. If no one wants to go, I will. Does anyone here need a bath?" Thomas asked.

"I'll go," Garret said as he climbed from the wagon.

Garrett noticed how dark it had become. The wind whipped the wagons and he calmed the horses by talking to them and holding the harnesses. He stood there holding them and the rain was running off the canvas roof. He was dry, but the water was flooding under the horses. Another clap of thunder, a flash of light and Garrett caught a glimpse of something or someone standing in the rain.

"Mr. Bach, I think I see someone in the woods?" Garrett whispered.

Thomas grabbed his colt from the wagon and jumped out the back.

"What are you talking about Garrett? Are you sure it's just not the wind in the trees?" Thomas asked.

"Just wait until the lightning strikes and look to the right, about 100 feet," Garret said.

They waited. When the lighting crackled, it lit up the woods. Thomas also could see someone standing there.

"Garrett get in this wagon. There is a rifle under the sacks. Wait until you hear from me. Nathan and Tucker, come take care of the horses. Kyle and Brian, take the rifles and watch the back and front of the wagon. If you hear shots, don't fire unless you can see who you are shooting at. It might be one of us," Thomas cautioned.

Thomas walked down the trail's edge, watching the timberline. Slowly he crepted along to where he saw the figure standing, Thomas looked at the ground and in the mud he could se tracks. They were headed toward the wagons. As Thomas stood up he heard,

"Don't move, Bach! Walk to the wagons. If you move, I'll kill you."

Thomas looked up it was Colonel Mitchell. He was holding his colt with his right hand and holding his side with the other.

"You're wounded. Let me help you," Thomas said.

"I think you have helped enough. Now, slowly lay your gun at my feet. Tell your kids to line up. All of them."

Thomas stood up and walked to the wagons. "Boys, put your guns down and come out of the wagon. Let's go."

The men walked as the rain got heaver. By the time they stood under the canvas, all the boys had exited the one wagon.

"Now, Bach. I'm it. I'm the only survivor of my whole regiment. Yes, I laid there playing dead while the Crow and the Siksika killed off my men. I laid there and listened to them talking about you and the boys. I heard the horn; I also head how you knew about this trap they were setting," the colonel ended as he leaned against the wagon. "I should just kill you right now, but you will hang once we reach Helena. In the meantime, where's the money?"

The boys looked at Thomas with a questioning look on their faces.

"Come on, Bach. Where's the money?" Mitchell demanded again.

"The money is gone. I gave it to the Crow and Siksika. There is no money," Thomas lied.

Mitchell grabbed Kyle. "Boy, you know about the money; don't you?"

"No, sir. I don't know about any money. I don't know what you are talking about," Kyle said.

"Fine, maybe I'll just have a look see," Mitchell looked into the one wagon. "Nothing but canvas and food."

Thomas started to edge his way closer to the end of the wagons.

"How about this one?" Mitchell pulled back the canvas and a gun barrel came out.

"Drop your weapon, Colonel!" Garret ordered.

The Colonel just stood there. "Oh, you think you have me do you. Boy you are not even wet behind your ears yet. Go ahead and shot me. Kill me boy!... See you can't do it."

With that Mitchell grabbed Kyle again and held his gun to the boy's head.

"Now, see when you shot me, I'll have just enough time to fire one shot into this boy's head. Now put down your gun. I said put down your gun!" Mitchell yelled wildly

Garrett put down his gun and stepped out of the wagon. Mitchell looked into the wagon and found the bags of money.

"Bach, I'm taking this wagon and all the money. I want you to stay here for two hours and I'll let you live, but I'm taking this boy. After

I get down to the base of the mountain I'll let him go. Now that's fair? Right?" Mitchell laughed evilly.

"Boys, hitch the horses up for the Colonel." Thomas instructed.

The Colonel and Kyle jumped into the front seat. If anyone tries anything, the boy is dead. Do we have an understanding, Bach?" Mitchell said as he slapped the reins and the wagon moved forward.

Thomas waited for the wagon to get about fifty feet. He took off running and jumped into the wagon. As the lightning lit up the sky, Thomas jumped into the front and grabbed a hold of the Colonel. The two rolled off the wagon and onto the ground. They rolled over the hill, then stopped. Mitchell started hitting Thomas in the face. Blood streamed from his mouth. Mitchell then pulled his knife from his side. He raised it high above his head and struck Thomas in the shoulder. Thomas screamed in pain as the knife tore into his flesh. Then like thunder Thomas heard a shot ring out. The Colonel straightened up, looked Thomas in the face and fell forward. Thomas slid out from under Mitchell's limp body. Then he looked up, there stood Garrett holding his rifle.

"Garrett, thank you! Help me up."

"Mr. Bach, are you hurt?" Garret asked.

"I'm fine. Where is Kyle?"

"He's okay He ran back to camp. Your shoulder is bleeding really bad. We need to get back to camp," Garret said.

As they stood up Garret asked, "Is he dead?"

Thomas walked up and knelt down beside the Colonel.

"Yes, he's dead. You did what you had to do. Now lets get back to the boys."

When they reached camp the other boys came running to help Thomas. Thomas took off his shirt and the bleeding had stopped. Kyle hugged Thomas. "I thought you were dead."

"No, just a little cut. Get in the wagon and get me the medicinal kit." Kyle placed some salve on Thomas's wound and the boys wrapped it with material. The boys started a fire and Thomas sat beside it, warming up his hands. The rain had stopped and it was getting dark.

"Boys, get the cooking pans out and let's make supper. We'll sleep here tonight and leave in the morning."

Thomas laid back and breathed in, "Do you smell that boys?"

"What are you talking about, Mr. Bach?" Nathan asked.

"One of the greatest smells in the world is when it's stopped raining. Everything is fresh and new. Clean. In the morning, we will get a fresh start. We will try to get to Chester by tomorrow's nightfall. Now, put the dry meat in the pot and there are some roots in a bag. I guess we are having stew tonight," Thomas smiled.

Thomas and the boys sat around the fire and ate stew and he told them the story. He told them of a great man named Regan Wright. The group traded stories until the fire had turned to just hot coals. They all bedded down for the night. Thomas leaned up against a tree and slept sitting up. His shoulder was sore, but the bleeding had stopped. He knew that with the rain, it was at least clean, but it was really painful. The night started to chill off, as Thomas looked to the sky. "Winter is just around the corner. You have done nothing to get Chester back to a town. But with this money, I think we can jump start it," He thought.

Morning came and Thomas was the first to rise. He stumbled up and his shoulder caught his attention. As he approached the boys, he could tell they were all sleeping soundly. Except he couldn't find Garrett. Thomas crossed down the trail until he heard the sound of digging. As he looked through the brush, Thomas could see Garrett putting the last few shovels of dirt on a grave.

"Well, I see you're up early, Garrett," Thomas said.

"Yes, sir. I couldn't sleep too good last night knowing that Mitchell was just laying up here. I wanted to give him a proper burial," Garrett said.

"Garrett, are you all right with what happened?" Thomas asked as he put his good hand on Garrett's shoulder.

"He's the first man that I've ever killed," Garrett said as he looked down at the grave. "But he's the only one that I thought I had to kill.

It all happened so fast; I really didn't have time to think," Garrett ended.

"You did what you had to do. And as far as I'm concerned, it wasn't your fault. He would have killed Kyle once he got down the road. He would have tried to kill all of us later. There's no telling what he would have said once he made it back to Chester," Thomas answered.

"The money. Why? What are you going to do with all that money? If it weren't for the money, I don't think he would have acted like he did," Garrett said facing Thomas.

"Ah, yes the money. Do you know what that money is to be used for?" Garrett shrugged his shoulders. "It's to be used to breathe life back into Chester. It will be used to set you boys up in your houses. The money is for everyone and everyone will get a fresh start. I would like to put my money in your bank once we get back and get everything setup. I think that is what your father and mother would have wanted, don't you?" Thomas asked.

"I guess so, but I really don't know much about banking. I mean, I can read and write and do math, but banking…I don't know?" Garrett hesitated.

"Don't worry. Once we get back and get settled, I'll send you to Helena to get trained. You can go to school and learn. The money isn't going anywhere. Now, let's get back to the others."

As Thomas and Garrett neared the camp, they noticed the others were still sleeping. Thomas yelled. "Are you boys going to sleep all day or are we going home?"

The boys sprang up and ran to Thomas. "Let's grab some bread and flat meat and break camp. Water the horses and off we go."

The rain had washed out most of the trail down the mountain. Thomas was glad when he reached the bottom. When they came to the fork in the road, Thomas stopped his wagon and started walking into the woods. The boys just stared at him wondering what he was doing. Thomas crossed to Mole's grave.

"Hey, mole, I just wanted to let you know that I found Jake and took care of him. I also just wanted to thank you for everything that you did for us. I also wanted to let you know that I'll be back this spring and when I come I'll bring you a proper headstone. Nancy and I are only a half day's ride from here, but with winter coming we won't see you till spring. I will not forget you Mole. Take care and God bless," Thomas turned to get up and saw Garrett was standing there.

"He's just an old friend I met along the trail. Just paying my respects," Thomas told Garrett.

"Well there is nothing wrong with that. The boys are watering the horses. We just used up the last of the feed for them. We need to get to grass before long. How much farther is it to Chester?" Garrett asked.

"Half a day, but we gotta get a move on. Kyle has a mom he needs to see and so do I," Thomas stated.

As the wagons moved on again, the horses seemed to pick up speed. They were on a road now; they would make up some time. As they approached a lower ridge, they could just make out the town from a distance. Thomas took out his scope and looked the town over. He could see people moving about through the streets. He saw children running around and men were working on houses. "What was going on he thought to himself? Well, there she is boys-Chester. We are about thirty minutes from her."

Kyle smiled as Thomas slapped the reins and yelled at the horses. They rode hard toward town. They entered through the side streets and slowed to a trot. They came upon Nancy's house and sat there. A young girl came to the front porch.

"Well, now, who do we have here?" Thomas asked.

"My name is Mary. And you are?" Mary asked.

"Why I'm Thomas Bach. Is Mrs. Bach home?"

Mary went running into the house and Thomas heard a scream and then everyone came running. Thomas climbed down off the wagon just in time to see Nancy come running through the door.

"Thomas! Oh my, Thomas!" Nancy said as she hugged and kissed him. "I thought you would never return!"

"Hey, I told you I'd be back." Thomas said as he held her tight. As they pulled away from each other, Nancy noticed blood on her shirt.

"Thomas, you are hurt? Are you all right? Oh, Thomas, I am just so happy to have you home again!"

"I'm fine, but I have brought you a little present," Thomas pulled back the canvas and Kyle stepped out.

"Kyle!"

"Mother!"

Nancy picked up Kyle and placed him on the ground and hugged him.

"You're alive. I missed you so!" Nancy cried.

"Mrs. Bach, you know what the doctor said about lifting anything. You know about your condition," David said.

"Condition? Are you sick?" Thomas asked.

"Not really. I'm pregnant, Thomas. I'm going to have your child," Nancy said as she hugged both Thomas and Kyle.

Thomas stood there with this blank look on his face. "How…When…a father!"

Thomas turned to the boys. "I'm going to be a father!"

It was then that both Nancy and Thomas saw all the children standing. "Well, we had better introduce everyone one." Thomas said. "Everyone in the house; we have a long night ahead of us."

Everyone gathered in the main room and talked. What had started out as just Thomas and Nancy was now a big, extended family. Garrett was talking to Mary and he spent most of the night talking to her. At the end of the night Thomas stood up.

"Boys, go out and get the bags." As the boys entered carrying the bags, Thomas said. "We are a large family. I want everyone here to stay together. To help get you started, I just want you to know that I have enough money to get everyone started. I want everyone to take up homes here. Boys open the bags." The boys dumped the bags out into a large pile. It was more money than everyone had ever seen.

"Thomas you found it! You found Regan's treasure!" Nancy exclaimed wonderingly.

"Yes, but I think that I have found something even better. I have found my life again. I have found what is really important to me and for all of us. It's here. It's this place, a place that we can call our own. We will take up roots here and may they run deep and wide." The children all clapped and tossed money in the air. "Now, let's eat and get this money put away," Thomas said.

That night as Thomas and Nancy talked about what had happened when both of them were apart. Thomas felt a fullness within himself. Something he had never felt before. He knew deep in his heart that they would make it. That the town would grow with the help of the young ones. Thomas placed his hand on Nancy's stomach.

"Our child grows within you. You know what this means, don't you?" Thomas asked.

"No what does it mean?" Nancy asked.

"It means that we have come full circle. Now all we have to do is grow old with each other. Life now will be boring in comparison. Can you deal with that? A life with a boring old man?" Thomas asked.

"Oh, I have a feeling that life with you, Thomas Bach, will be anything but boring. What do you think, Laura?" Nancy said laughing.

"I think everyone is now a family and we have each other," Laura said.

"And I think that in the morning we find you your own bed to sleep in. How's that sound? Laura? Laura?" Thomas said.

"She can't hear you; she's asleep. Now hold me and never let me go, Mr. Bach!" Nancy demanded.

"Sure but where is our bear skin?" Thomas asked laughing, as he blew out the candle.

CPSIA information can be obtained at www.ICGtesting.com
Printed in the USA
BVOW09s2047180214

345312BV00001B/90/P

9 781606 721636